All Those Buckles

ABCDEFGHIJKLMNOP

ALL THOSE BUCKLES

E. R. GAGGIN

Illustrated by
MILDRED CLOETE

NEW YORK · THE VIKING PRESS
1945

COPYRIGHT 1945 BY E. R. GAGGIN

FIRST PUBLISHED BY THE VIKING PRESS IN MAY 1945

PUBLISHED ON THE SAME DAY IN THE DOMINION OF CANADA BY

THE MACMILLAN COMPANY OF CANADA LIMITED

SECOND PRINTING NOVEMBER 1945

PRINTED IN THE UNITED STATES OF AMERICA

To

Eddy

Contents

Contents

All Those Buckles

1. An Alphabet Should Live on a Hillside

M R. WATSON owned the largest farm between Cliffton
Center and Riverhead. It bogged and squished
through swales and beside lovely bays along the shore of
the St. Lawrence River, it climbed over old gray rock up
slanting pastures to where jack pines sighed in the sun and
groaned in the gales, it touched on cool stretches of water
lilies and hot patches of pink dogbane, and in one corner,
aided by a snaggy old butternut tree, a few feet of Mr.
Watson's farm concealed a ridiculously tiny tenant house
under a tangle of wild grape vines and snowberry bushes.
An almost forgotten little tenant house until the army
came to the north country looking for a site for an airfield one day and finding what they wanted just where
Abijah Buckle lived, on the flatlands outside of Cliffton
Center.

Then Mr. Watson, who couldn't allow the best foreman he had ever had on the farm turned right out of his
own home with all his family to camp along the river

shore, did some pretty quick remembering. He remembered the little tenant house. More than that, on a Wednesday in July when the Buckles were obliged to give up their nice flat fields for the army's use, Mr. Watson sent four farm wagons to move them to the little tenant house in its smother of wild grape vines and snowberry bushes. And he sent his three best men, Jim Hopkins, Fred Johnson, and Chuck Floyd, to drive three of the wagons. Abijah Buckle drove the fourth himself—the one that looked as if it had been decorated for the County Fair with huge golden dandelion blossoms all around the rail. All those Buckles had heads like bursting dandelions and they ringed the rail, eager to have a look at their new home.

Fan was the first to speak. She always was. "Where are you going to put Imogene, Charles?" she asked.

Mrs. Buckle chuckled. "Now, now, sweety," she warned. "Don't let's begin looking for trouble. After all, this will be only for a day or two, just until Mr. Watson finds us a bigger place."

Fan stood on a covered basket and took another searching look at the snowberry bushes. "I asked you where you are going to put that calf, Charles," she repeated.

Mrs. Buckle suggested a rope and the butternut tree but Fan wafted that idea aside. "Imogene has always been accustomed to very nice barns," she said primly. "Julia and Katy and Lulu could sleep tonight in their covered basket, maybe, though how that little duck is going to get

along without her swim is something I don't know. Do you see any brook inside those bushes, Delia?"

Delia didn't. Nor did Charles, Eddy, George, or little Horace. "Dusty as a flour bin," they all agreed.

"What kind of a place is this for all us Buckles?" Fan stepped down from the covered basket. "A family that is as long as an alphabet."

"Mercy, not quite, deary," laughed Mrs. Buckle.

"Well, we go from A-is-Abijah to B-is-Bessie, C-is-Charles——"

"I know. And D-is-Delia and E-is-Eddy."

"Clear down to L-is-Lulu chicken. That's a pretty good start." Nobody disputed Fan this time. "A family that is an alphabet should live on a hillside so the army wouldn't want their farm for an airfield," she explained.

"I know," Mrs. Buckle agreed. "But Mr. Watson will find us another place for a home, and if we can help in this war by giving the army a nice flat airfield we should be proud to do it, deary."

"Mr. Jole wasn't. He had the only place to rent in The Center big enough and what did he say? 'Not to all those Buckles!' That's what he said. Do you call that helping?"

Jim called out just then to say that he and Fred had the stove set up, the shutters knocked off the kitchen window, and now, since there was so little space inside, they were of the opinion that the best thing would be for the wagons to turn back to Watson's barn, with what was left in them, and wait for morning.

"Abijah's going back with us, too," he added. "Mr. Watson thinks it will be better for him to spend the night at the big house so they can both get an early start house-hunting tomorrow morning. It might take most of the forenoon. We'll take your calf too and that basket of duck and chicks, if you like."

Fan declined the offer promptly. "We Buckles like to stay together," she said.

The wagons rumbled away then, and the Buckles were together—together, but alone, in the little tenant house among the snowberry bushes. And in nobody's memory had they been so quiet. That is, until little Horace lifted his voice in the howl that he kept for very special occasions.

"I want to go back!" he told the world. "I want to go back to my very own home!"

"You haven't got any very own home any more; the army's got it for an airfield. I expect by now the porches are all torn off, and the roof maybe, and—" Fan stopped, not because her imagination was running down but because it looked as if Horace was close to an explosion. "Hey, Horace, you can have this little house," she offered gently. "Mr. Watson said so."

"I don't want it. It hasn't even got a door to it."

The little house among the snowberry bushes didn't even have a door? Fourteen startled eyes confirmed that fact. "Jim took it off to get the stove inside, I bet you," said Fan. "Likely it's back in Mr. Watson's barn by now."

"No, it isn't. It's under the butternut tree." Just because Horace kept his eyes open and knew what was going on he didn't have to like everything, he hoped. "I'm not going to sleep in a house with the door outside under a tree."

The time had come for action and Mrs. Buckle took it. "You're going to sleep inside here tonight, door or no door, and like it, Horace deary," she said. "But first, you're going to eat inside here. It has been quite a day for all of us and we need food and rest. Feel under that heap of quilts in the corner, Delia lovey, and find the pail of baked beans. They'll be warm enough. Then you and Charles bring all the cushions and blankets inside. Eddy, you fetch the big mirror and brace it up against a wall inside somewhere. George and Fan, you begin with the blue dishes that Aunty Belle gave us for Christmas."

"Me?" George couldn't believe his ears. "Suppose I dropped one?"

"You'd just better not," his twin was the first to warn him. "You know Aunty Belle! Where'll we put Julia, Katy, and Lulu, Mother?" she asked after a second glance around the little tenant house. "Somebody'll step on 'em."

"Leave them in their basket, deary. Shove it under the sink." Mrs. Buckle may have had problems of her own at that moment, but no shadow of them darkened her merry face. "They won't mind for one night, I promise you," she added briskly. "Now let me see, Horace and I will have the bed in the other room——"

"There's only one other room," Horace interrupted bitterly.

"Which is what we will have," his mother assured him. "Fan and Delia will have a mattress behind the screen in the corner. George, Eddy, and Charles can cuddle down on cushions in the kitchen wherever there's no furniture."

"Katy and Lulu never slept with George before."

"It'll be quite a treat for the chicks, Fan, and for that little Julia duck, too." Mrs. Buckle smiled and the circle of small, bewildered faces smiled with her. "Now for beans," she ordered. And then, "Oh, look at the doorway, Horace Buckle," she whispered. "Who would want a door between us and that? Silvery moonlight on the dangling vines, making the funniest shadows for us to watch, and two chipmunks dancing on the sill!"

The twins, Fan and George, pushed through the snow-berry bushes and entered the kitchen of the little tenant house a long, restful night and a few early morning hours later. Mrs. Buckle was making ready to stir up a johnny-cake in her yellow mixing bowl. "You'll have to keep Julia and Katy and Lulu in here, Mother." Fan sighed and wiped her hot, dusty face on the knee of her pink sunsuit. "They don't like it outside."

"No?"

"They run like sixty-seven grasshoppers," groaned George. "Of course, Julia is running to find some bath water, but what Katy and Lulu think they are after beats me. Where's Charles? And Delia? And everybody?" he added, curiously.

"Charles and Delia have gone up to the big house for eggs and milk, deary."

"Then that means George and I will have to feed Imo-gene!" Fan sat down upon the covered basket wearily. "A smart thing you did, George Buckle, when you told Mr. Watson about Vics, and Chests of Cheer, and every-thing."

"I didn't tell him about everything."

"What did you leave out?"

George couldn't think at the moment. "All I said, when I asked him did he have a job for me this summer———"

"I know that much. And all he said was, 'What kind of a job?' It was after that when you really broke down."

"I did not. I just told him that Delia earned twenty-five

cents washing dishes; an' Charles earned a dollar running errands for Downe's Drug Store; an' Eddy——"

"What did Eddy earn?" Fan giggled disdainfully.

"He says that he's going to earn more money than any of us when he gets around to it."

"Uh-huh, when!" Fan stood up, moved behind the kitchen table and, reaching inside a can, helped herself to a chunk of brown sugar. "You told him how you an' me an' little Horace weeded onions for a whole afternoon for Mr. King, didn't you? An' all he paid us was a quarter an' five cents for little Horace. An' Horace was so mad he threw all the weeds back on——"

"But I told Mr. Watson no more onions!" George added hastily. Those hours in Mr. King's onion patch were no golden memory to him, either.

Fan sniffed. "A lucky thing you did," she said. "Anyway, why did you have to tell him about the Chests of Cheer?"

"He asked me why all the Buckles were so busy making money all of a sudden and I said that Miss Lettice, at our school, was packing Chests full of Cheer for the poor people over where the war is and we had to fill 'em. All the kids in school earn something an' she buys stuff with the money an' the Buckles have earned more than anybody else."

"Go on. Go right on from there."

"Well, I said that we could earn still more if we had some Vics."

"Now you can stop. You told him about Vics!"

"But did I know that right away he'd go and give us four?" George had a real grievance here, and he aired it with vigor. Nobody could have been prepared for such munificence, he felt. "I told him that the Canadian children across the border have one turkey, or one pig, or one calf, or one something from the farm and they call it their 'Vic' and they raise it themselves and then they sell it and send what money they make to the poor people over where the war is."

"And right away he gives you four."

"Imogene, Julia, Katy, and Lulu. Gosh!"

"You said it. All they do is eat and quack for a bath. The war could be over before Imogene could learn how to make milk for us to sell. An' if Katy an' Lulu ever lay eggs, they'll be sparrows' eggs, and a cent a dozen, I bet you. Where did little Horace and Eddy go, Mother?"

"Little Horace found something out under the butternut tree to play with, lovey. And Eddy went to The Center."

For one moment the silence was heavy in the kitchen of the little tenant house. Then it was broken. Splintered. "To The Center?" roared George. "If Eddy Buckle went to The Center he went to Bandlo's Circus. He was saying yesterday that maybe he might go today, and then Jim drove up with the first farm wagon and we had to move and he didn't say any more. But I didn't think he'd go off by himself."

"Where'd he get the money?" shrilled Fan, drawing attention to the real importance of Eddy's misdeed. "Eddy didn't have any little money in his bank. All he had was that big chunk that Aunty Belle gave him on his birthday 'cause he was quiet when he came to see her, an' wiped his feet on the mat, an' didn't spill things on her tablecloth. How much was it, Mother?"

"Ten dollars, sweety."

"Did Eddy take ten dollars to Bandlo's Circus?"

"Well, it was his, Fan."

"It belonged to the Chests to buy stuff for the poor people over where the—oh my goodness gracious, look what Horace has got." With great presence of mind, Fan drew George close to her side behind the kitchen table and then, dropping to her knees, hauled the covered basket to safety. Deciding that she could see all that was necessary from that position, she remained where she was, crouched behind the basket. "Is that a wild cat, Horace?" she quavered.

"Not now, he isn't." Little Horace was the calmest Buckle in the kitchen at the moment. "I don't know what he was at first, but he started to get fresh an' I pulled him down out of the butternut tree by his tail."

"What made you do that, Horace?"

" 'Cause that was all I could get hold of. He wanted to run away, but I said, 'No, sir, I'm going to show you to Eddy. You come right back down out of that tree.' And he did."

"I'll bet." George looked and shivered. "That cat's bigger 'n you are, Horace."

"Uh-huh. An' you ought to hear him scree-ee-eeowl. Eddy likes animals an' there's an awful lot of cat here for him to play with, if he wants to."

"That's the biggest and blackest cat in the whole world," Fan agreed, and drew nearer her mother's protecting arm. "What's he doing? Hey, don't let him sharpen his claws on our kitchen stool, Horace."

Little Horace cuffed the monster's ears boldly, holding him by his leather collar and locket to do it, while the twins watched and shivered.

"Stand hard on top of the covered basket, George," Fan urged uneasily.

> There once was a black cat named Vaughn
> Who was black as two nights before dawn;
> He dined on a duck,
> And a chicken for luck,
> Then went out and had fits on our lawn.

Is that cat's name Vaughn, do you know, Horace?"

Mrs. Buckle stopped kneading butter into cornmeal and, stooping, snapped her fingers invitingly toward the stranger. "Come on, old chap," she said pleasantly. "Let's be friends."

The cat took his time about it. A gentleman who has just had his tail loosened at the roots shouldn't be expected to get over the affront in a hurry. He glared at Fan, he lifted his mustachios and spat at Horace, he swelled his tail like a cleaning brush and swung it once in George's direction and then, having the lesser Buckles where he wanted them, he approached Mrs. Buckle and licked her outstretched hand delicately. Butter! These fingers smelled of butter, they tasted of butter—anybody could see that this cat liked butter. He settled down to a thorough wash-up. But while he was busy with one of her hands, Mrs. Buckle flipped his locket open with the other and discovered his name.

"Oliver Binns." She spelled the letters out slowly. "I don't know any Binns family in The Center."

"Nobody in our school is named Binns, either," said Fan.

"And this is the only house between The Center and Riverhead except that place just before you get to The Center, that Shady Rest Cabins, Hamburgers, Antiques place. And the man who lives there is Mr. Wente. There isn't any Binns family around here." George was convinced of the fact, but Fan was thinking.

"This isn't the only house between The Center and Riverside. George," she said after a moment. "There's Braeside."

"Braeside?"

"That funny little street where you turn off the County Road by the store and go down to the dock, to the river. There are seven houses and the store on that street, four on one side and four on the other and Mrs. Watson said the Braeside folks were going to seed like their petunias. What did she mean by that, Mother?"

"I couldn't say, deary. Where did you ever learn so much about Braeside?"

"I went to the store with her once to get some fish an' the man 'most ate us up. He thought we wanted bass, but when Mrs. Watson said codfish he kind of calmed down."

"What's wrong with bass?" asked George.

"There's a law or something. You can't sell 'em in stores near the river. Maybe it was that, or maybe it was just that he didn't like children."

"Aw phooey. Who wouldn't like children?"

"Lots of old people don't. Mr. Jole doesn't, you know. And the Braeside folks don't. It could be 'cause they don't know 'em very well. But there's that Sam Cooter in our school, I wouldn't like that boy even if I knew him well enough to. Sam Cooter is a— Hey, Horace, keep a good hold on Vaughn's tail."

"I am."

It was surprising how much Fan could see of the room from her refuge behind the covered basket under the kitchen table. The black cat yawned and she waited until he was finished with that and had had a good stretch before continuing with the story of Braeside.

"You never saw such a messy street, Mother," she said.

"Messy, deary? What do you mean?"

"Garden trash all over the place. The folks clip their hedges and trim their hollyhocks and pull up their petunias and just toss the stuff over into the street, I guess. What do they care, they don't have to walk in it. There's no place to walk, really, except down to the dock at the other end and they take the middle of the road for that. Mr. Moom lives down there just above the dock, right over the river."

"Mr. Moom? Do you mean the Mr. Moom in the bank at The Center, Fan?"

"Uh-huh. He lives in Braeside. In the last house."

"Well, no wonder you had me all mixed up for a minute with your talk about 'Braeside.' I never heard the place called that." Mrs. Buckle dipped both arms to the elbows in a pan of hot suds and had a good scrub. "We always called it 'Mr. Moom's Street.' Your father and Charles and Delia—Delia was the baby, then—and I had the grandest picnic there one day. Right alongside the swale, just before you turn into Mr. Moom's Street. We didn't go any farther. But I'll never forget the redwings whistling in the reeds. And all about kingfishers were darting, their beaks bristling with minnows. And overhead were terns tumbling in the sunshine like a skyful of silvery new moons. There was a slanting pasture back of the swale and clear up to the very top where it bumped against a pine woods it was white as white with daisies, blue as blue with harebells, and pink as pink with dogbane, willow herb, and meadow-sweet."

Fan came up from behind the covered basket and rested her chin on the kitchen table, close to the mixing bowl. "I wish the swale had been all pink," she sighed. "I like pink things the very best of all."

"You would have liked the rest, sweety." Mrs. Buckle reached for the butter dish. "The elderberries with their black fruit umbrellas held high, wide, and handsome in the breezes; and the silky dogwoods with clusters of heavenly-blue berries that looked as if somebody had dusted them with powdered silver; and the wild honeysuckles with fruit like coral drops; and the Long-purples. There's something pink for you, Fan, a whole, flaming patch of Long-purples."

Fan pushed the cornmeal box out of the way and eyed the Buckles' morning caller nervously. "I hope he doesn't live in Braeside," she said. "It would be just like him to."

"What do you care?" Horace wanted to know. "You don't have to live there. Somebody's coming down the road."

Two golden heads bloomed behind the kitchen table. "Is it Mr. Watson's car?" asked George. And then, in almost the same breath, "No, it rattles too much."

"And it's coming from The Center," Fan added, standing on her tiptoes but seeing no more than before. "Mr. Watson wouldn't be coming from The Center. We know there is only one empty farm there and Mr. Jole said, 'Not all those Buckles.' To send him the war, but not all those Buckles! Mr. Watson would be coming from Riverhead."

"Well, this is coming from The Center, all right," George was certain of that now.

"An' it rattles 'cause it's a circus," added Horace, as if a circus was the most matter-of-fact thing in the world.

George and Fan knew that it wasn't. They came out from behind the table and slid straight for the doorway with a rush that decided Mr. Oliver Binns to end his call than and there, in one piece if possible. But to end it, tail or no tail. He jerked free of little Horace's detaining hand and, leaping for the butternut tree, walked straight up it to hide among the thickest branches. Away up. It would have been a great relief to him could he have known that he was forgotten at once and completely by the golden-headed Buckles below.

"It's a circus, all right," said Fan. "Roman chariot and camel and everything."

"That's no camel." George knew what he knew, but no more. "It's got too many ridges. Mother, what is it that's got one hump right after another clear down to its tail?"

"That looks like a poor old abused horse to me, deary."

"A horse? Who's driving it?"

"Eddy," Horace told them calmly.

"Eddy? Eddy Buckle?" Fan quivered under the shock —until George's words of but a few moments ago rang a bell in her memory. "Law me, Eddy said that he would earn more money than any of us when he got around to it. Mother, do you suppose that he could get around to it with an old camel-horse like that?"

2. Mark

"I'D like to see Eddy Buckle try to get that old horse into one of Miss Lettice's Chests of Cheer," giggled George, just as Charles and Delia breezed through the snowberry bushes with the news that Eddy was approaching the little tenant house in the clown's chariot from Bandlo's Circus and that he was driving that old sneezer.

"Sneezer?" asked Mrs. Buckle.

"Ye-ah. MAGGIE." Charles took over. "That's the trick horse," he explained breathlessly. "Every time the band begins to play, 'When you and I were young, MAGGIE,' all the drums and things blare out something awful on the Maggie an'——"

"Why?" asked Fan who liked her details as she went along.

"Because that's his trick. Just as soon as he hears MAGGIE he sneezes. And the clown hops out of the chariot with a bottle of cough syrup as big as a milk pail, and he says, 'Poor, poor Maggie,' and nothing happens. Then he says, 'Poor, poor MAGGIE!' And poof, that old horse sneezes the syrup bottle right out of the clown's hand and it goes sailing away. It's a balloon, really. Anyway, Sam Cooter said so and he ought to know. He worked for Bandlo's last week."

"Sam Cooter did?" Fan couldn't believe it. "What did he do?"

"Helped the magician. That's really Mr. Bandlo, you know, with his tall silk hat on. Sam scrouged under a little table and put things in the hat for the magician."

"What things?"

"Well, he was supposed to put bunnies in, mostly. But once he put in a little green snake and Mr. Bandlo went up like a rocket and when he came down he kicked the basket that was under the table and bunnies snowed down all over the place and Sam lost his job."

"And that's just exactly what Eddy Buckle has got, I bet you," cried Fan suddenly, adding two and two to make a perfect four. "Sam's job. He's coming to tell us that he is working for Mr. Bandlo, that he has got around to making more money than all the rest of us, that—law me, I should think Eddy would be ashamed of driving a cart with a bare man on it!"

"He isn't all bare." Delia was shocked, too, but just. "He's kind of wrapped around in a pink nightgown."

"A pink nightgown is no better than skin on a fat man, Delia. Look right back of the horse's tail on the front of the cart, Mother."

"I am, sweety. But I'm trying to hear what Eddy is saying too. He wants something."

Out of the sudden silence Eddy was heard demanding

assistance. "Mr. Bandlo didn't tell me how to make him stop," he called. "He slapped him to start him off, but now he won't stop for me. Grab hold of his collar, Charles, then all of you hang on and bear down like sixty. That ought to brake him. He hasn't got much strength yet."

"Poof, that one and his strength." Fan was disgusted. "He'll stop for me, I bet you." And then with all her lung power, which was considerable when she felt called upon to use it to the full, she yelled but one sharp word. "MAGGIE!"

The ridgy horse stopped. No doubt about it, he stopped. But first he sneezed so hard that Eddy, who was taken entirely unawares, toppled backward out of the little chariot into the ditch and little Horace who was directly in the tornado's path was blown into a tangle of folds in his mother's apron. Bandlo's horse's sneeze, the Buckles saw, had not been overrated.

It was the little chariot, however, that gave Eddy cause for serious thought. He picked himself out of the ditch and surveyed it critically. "I might have known there was a hitch somewhere," he sniffed, "or old Bandlo wouldn't have thrown it in. No back to it, I'll have to get some slats and nail a back on there the very first thing I do. I might get tired of being tossed out on my ear every time I wanted to stop."

"What'll I do with him, Eddy?" asked Charles who had managed to catch hold of a rope that was swinging from the horse's collar. "Will he run away?"

"He won't even walk away now. Once he has stopped he's the tiredest horse I ever saw. Tie him to the butternut tree along with Imogene; he won't bother her. He'll go to sleep just as soon as he finds something to lean against. Only don't you ever do that again, Fan Buckle."

"Do what?"

"Yell his name right out."

"What'll I call him, then?"

"You can say, 'Mag-you-know-who.' "

"I'd rather not speak to her. When are you going to take her back to Bandlo's, Eddy Buckle? Mr. Watson won't like it if he drives up for us and finds he has to wait while you——"

"He won't have to wait," Eddy interrupted coldly. "This is my horse. I bought him."

"You bought,—hey, did you take that ten dollars that was going to help poor people over where the war is and buy an old sneezer that you can't even speak her name? Have to call her 'Mag-you-know-who' so she won't guess who you're talking about. A fine thing!"

"If she's got a cold, Eddy," said Delia, the gentle and helpful, "I could cure it. Mr. Watson showed me how to make a warm mash with lobelia in it."

"He hasn't got any cold. That sneezing is his trick. And this horse is a he, no matter about his name. I could change that." Eddy turned a cold stare on his sisters which Fan overlooked completely. "All Bandlo's animals are ridgy," he explained. "They are pretty nearly starved, that's why.

Mr. Bandlo doesn't care. He said he was sick of circuses, anyway, and just about ready to sell out to the nearest boneyard and try his hand at raising pears in Oregon. I almost bought the dancing pig, but there was more to Mag-you-know-who, especially after Mr. Bandlo threw the chariot into the bargain. I never noticed about the back being gone, then."

"I'm s'prised," said Fan, as if she really meant it. "You never noticed about your Chest money being gone either, did you?"

"I'll make plenty when I get around to it. More than all the rest of you."

"More than ten dollars?"

"A good deal more. I might even take over a whole Chest, just for myself."

"Mother!" Fan dropped financial matters for the moment. "Do we have to have a fat man in a pink nightgown in our family?" she asked bitterly. Most of the Buckles, it was easily seen, were with her at heart. All except Eddy.

"That isn't an old fat man, Fan Buckle," he said proudly. "That is a king by the name of Nero."

"I don't like him. Nero, phooey! How are you going to make money with him? Run a circus?"

Mrs. Buckle stilled the rising storm. "Hus-s-sh!" she said. "Let Eddy tell us how Mr. Bandlo came to sell him a horse and chariot. That's what I am curious about."

"Why, it was just after the police came into the tent while I was handing up bunnies."

"Did you get Sam Cooter's job?" asked Fan.

"Did you say police, deary?" echoed his mother.

"Yes." It was Eddy's reply to both. "While I was under the table somebody ran behind a screen and said, 'Hist, boss, the cops!' An' Mr. Bandlo said, 'Out of my path, bunnies. I'm on my way to Oregon.' And then the clown behind the screen said, 'I'll take the pig for Sunday dinner, but what about the horse?' An' I was still under the table, you know, but Mr. Bandlo heard me when I whispered, 'I'll buy Mag-you-know-who.' "

"I'll bet he did, lovey."

"He reached under the tablecloth an' dragged me right outside the tent with him an' he asked me how much money I had on me, an' what do you know, ten dollars was just the price he was asking for that horse."

"If you'd have had twenty-five cents more the price would have been ten twenty-five," said Charles shrewdly.

"I did have twenty-five cents more."

"Get out! And old Bandlo let you off with it?"

"He didn't know about it and he was in a hurry, you see. He tossed me into Nero, grabbed my ten-dollar bill, and gave Mag-you-know-who an awful wallop to wake him up and start him off down the road. He yelled after me that if the horse dropped dead before I got out of town I could sell his skin and bones to the boneyard. Do you know, I don't like Mr. Bandlo, Mother. I'll never work for him again."

"No, lovey, you'll never work for him again."

"Where's the quarter, Eddy?" asked Fan suddenly. "At least you've got that much for the Chests."

"I spent it."

Now, here was a problem that set everybody's head aspinning. How could anyone spend twenty-five cents while he was driving along the County Road behind a horse that wouldn't stop?

"How did you spend it?" asked Fan simply. "How could you?"

"Why, just as we got in front of Shady Rest Cabins, Hamburgers, Antiques, Mag-you-know-who kind of sagged and Mr. Wente came out and said that anybody could see that he was starving, so I bought him a double hamburger."

"My heavens, feeding that old ridgy horse like a prince while all the poor people over where the war is——"

"I'll get around to them pretty soon," Eddy promised briskly. "What I've got to do now is to cure this sneezing."

"Lobelia, Eddy." Delia pushed through the swarm of family but stopped at Eddy's vigorous headshaking.

"He hasn't got a cold, I told you," her brother told her all over again. "Nobody ever taught him how to stop running or how to start off running the right way; that's all that ails him. Of course, he'll stop when he smells hamburgers, or when somebody yells Mag-you-know-what. And he'll go when you give him a good slap on the drumstick like Mr. Bandlo and Mr. Wente did. But I might not always have an extra quarter, and you bet I don't always

want to be tossed out of Nero after a sneeze, and somebody might not be near to slap him. I've got to change his name. And then teach him about whoa and giddap. I might call him MacArthur."

The Buckles exploded all among the snowberry bushes. Nothing had ever shocked them quite like this. "Why-y-y-y, Eddy Buckle, you can't do that," shrilled Fan over and over again. "You simply can't do that."

"I should say not," echoed Delia, the gentle Delia, almost as wildly. "Tell him that he can't do that, Mother."

"If you were a hero how would you like to have Bandlo's horse named after you?" demanded Charles.

"It would serve him right. Let's call the old nag 'Ed,' " added George bitterly.

Little Horace tittered contemptuously, nor did he exclude Nero from his scoffing. He tossed a clod of earth against the Roman chariot speckling the pink nightgown from hem to hem.

"Now see what you've done to N." Eddy stood on his toes, brushed aside a few stray hairs from Mag-you-know-who's tail, and exposed the full front of the cart to the Buckles' view. "Is that a nice way to treat a Vic?" he demanded. "One of our very own Alphabet Helpers."

If the Buckles were shocked before, they were staggered at these words. "That thing in our family?" Fan found her voice first. "Mother!"

"Listen, sweety. Eddy is trying to tell us about it."

Eddy was. "We Buckles are an alphabet," he explained

soberly. "From A-is-Abijah to H-is-Horace. That much we did all by ourselves. And then came this war, and the Vics, and we went down to L-is-Lulu. And there we stuck, 'cause I didn't have any Vic of my own. But just as soon as I saw Mag-you-know-who, I said, 'There's our M-is-something.' I knew I'd have to find another M name, of course. And then when Mr. Bandlo gave me the cart, why it was just like Fate. There it was, L-is-Lulu, M-is-MacArthur-maybe, and N-is-Nero."

"You could call him Mark, Eddy," said Fan, testing the name doubtfully.

"Mark?"

"Mark?" echoed the Buckles. "What Mark?"

"Mr. Mark Watson. I don't believe he'd feel insulted, but if he did you could weed onions for him until he got over it."

Honk!

The Buckles turned from the butternut tree and faced in the direction of Riverhead. Honk! Honk! Two more times. Father and Mr. Watson were coming. Mr. Watson had found them a new home and was coming to move them. The big shiny car moved easily up to the little tenant house and stopped with a shocked squeal. Mr. Buckle leaned over the wheel as if he felt faint all of a sudden, but Mr. Watson hopped outside where he had more room to stare.

"What in the world?" he shouted. "What in the world is that?"

"That's a horse, sir," George explained. "Fan just named him after you."

"Because Eddy thinks he's such a good horse," added Fan, delicately.

"Where did he come from?"

"From Bandlo's. Is he a good horse, sir? He'd better be, 'cause Eddy's got ten dollars and a quarter tied up in him. The quarter was for a hamburger to give him strength to get out here from The Center."

"Are you, by any chance, talking of Bandlo's Circus, Fan?" asked Mr. Watson, wiping his forehead. As if that was enough to wipe the bewilderment out of his brain! "Bandlo's Trained Animal Show that is performing in The Center?"

"Sure. Mark is the sneezing horse. Boy-y-y, can he sneeze!"

"A man who treats an animal like that ought to be in jail," said Mr. Watson solemnly. "And I expect Bandlo is, by this time. At least, we heard in Riverhead that the state police——"

"Pooh! He got away from them. He's on his way to Oregon now to raise pears."

"To—to what? Well, sir, if you want to know anything, just ask those Buckles is what I always say. You run up to the house, Eddy, and bring Jim back with you. Tell him we need some quick advice on how to save a horse. Jim Hopkins is the best vet in the north country and he'll have —he'll have——"

• "Mark." Fan helped him out.

"I hate to say it." Mr. Watson grinned and winked at Abijah Buckle. "But then, I suppose it was meant to be a compliment?" He looked inquiringly around the circle of wide blue, honest eyes.

"It was because he had to be an M-horse," Fan explained when nobody else felt like it. "To come after L-is-Lulu. But it's better than if that chariot had to be an M-thing. We never would have named that fat pink man 'Mark.' "

"I hope you think better of me than that." Mr. Watson wiped his forehead again. "But get Jim down here, Eddy. He'll have my namesake on his feet and sneezing again in jig time, if the job can be done at all."

"Did you get a new house for us, sir?" asked George, out of the blue.

Five golden heads were shocked to see Mr. Watson shake his head drearily. More shocked at his words. "Nary a house," he acknowledged. "Not even a chicken coop. Just as soon as the folks learned that we were after a place for 'All those Buckles'——"

"Law me, what made you tell them about the chicks?"

"I didn't, pink dot. 'Chicken coop' was only a byword."

And then all those Buckles stood very still to hear what Mr. Watson was saying to Mother.

"Chuck brought the message to the farm just before I started out on this house-hunting business this morning," he said. "Another shipload of war children are expected at

some port across the border today. Our share will get into
Gananoque tomorrow, and being on the welcoming committee I'm expected there to see that they are placed in
the proper homes. It's a tough deal for you, Bessie."

"Oh bosh! Don't let's mention 'tough deal' in connec-
tion with the Buckles; not in the same breath with what
those poor little children have been through."

"I know. But still, leaving you here under a butternut
tree, no neighbors, no store, no——"

"Well-l, phooey on 'em!" George, possessing a one-
track mind, was still dealing mentally with the landowners
of Riverhead and Cliffton Center. " 'All those Buckles,' "
he repeated bitterly. "Anybody'd think we'd hurt their old
houses. Gosh, we had a house once so good that—well,
it was so good that the army wanted it. I guess that
ought to show 'em. Why don't you build us another house,
Mr. Watson? You've got lots of land around here that
even the cows don't want, I bet you."

Mr. Watson started to laugh, thought better of it, and
clapped his fist on George's shoulder. "You've got something there, my lad, bless me if you haven't," he boomed.
"After all, why should I waste time flying hither and yon,
begging fools to rent to my foreman, when I own about
all the vacant land in the north country? That is a matter
I'll attend to as soon as I get back from Gananoque."

"Tomorrow, sir?"

"Well, you can't set a clock by the way ships move
across the ocean nowadays. I hope it will be tomorrow, but

your father and I might be held there another day. What worries me is leaving you packed like—hey, I've got an idea. This is my house, and that lot belongs to me! Right in the midst of nice neighbors, too. Charles, you run up to the farm and catch Eddy and Jim before they leave the barns. Tell Jim to bring the tractor along with his medical kit and about a keg of oats, and the biggest trailer, some rollers, and all the men on the place."

Mrs. Buckle had to know more about an order like this. "I've got a johnnycake in the oven, Mark," she warned. "This sounds to me like an idea that might not be too good for baking."

"If the johnnycake falls I'll eat it," Mr. Watson promised her handsomely. "This sardine can full of Buckles must be located in a safe spot, near a store, near neighbors, near kindly help before night. The men will roll you, house and all, onto the trailer, start up the tractor, and haul you to——"

"Where?" asked Fan, suspiciously.

"Why, to a vacant lot I own down the road, near the Braeside store."

"Braeside!" Fan rose to her toes and spun like a disturbed wasp. "I knew he was going to say 'Braeside.' You tell him, Mother, what the Braeside folks would say if they saw 'All those Buckles' come rolling down their road. And the Vics. Law me, the Vics, most of all."

"You don't really mean Mr. Moom's Street, do you, Mark?" asked Mrs. Buckle thoughtfully.

"Well, Moom does live in Braeside. But what has that to do with it? He lives in the last house on one side, right above the dock. My vacant lot is across the way. You'll have a quaint old party by the name of Miss Tissy for your next-door-neighbor. And you'll be near Bill Hanley's store and a phone."

"But they don't like children in Braeside," cried Fan to deaf ears after little Horace had announced that the tractor was approaching. "Hi, Jim!" he piped. "Don't forget the door this time!"

"Door? What door?"

Horace waved both pointing arms and then, easing in between Imogene and Nero, kicked the door smartly. "That one," he said. "It belongs on the kitchen. Gosh, the chipmunks that came inside last night and crawled all over my feet."

Jim was ashamed of himself and said so over and over again. "You folks jammed in here like seven wrens in a teacup," he lamented. "And no door to the place."

"There's a front door," Horace admitted. "We shut that, but no good! Chipmunks are back-door folks, I guess."

"Well, take the front door off, Fred, and stack it up under the tree with the other one before something happens to it." Jim leaned down from his seat in the tractor to shout more orders to the men. "The steps, too. Take them off and pile them next to the doors. And see that we don't forget anything this time."

The little tenant house protested vigorously against being pulled by a tractor from its snowberry bushes and wild grape vines. It creaked and snapped and shook a few more bricks down its chimney. Nothing like this should happen to a house as old as it was, it felt. But after a while, when it was perched comfortably on the trailer with golden-headed Buckles boiling out of the windows and doorways and not even the red geranium in the kitchen window upset, it began to think that traveling might be fun, after all.

"We're a regular p'rade," cried George as the tractor bumped across the ditch onto the County Road.

The rest of the Buckles agreed that they were, indeed, a real parade. Mr. Watson's car led the way; close behind it came the snorting tractor and the farm hands; behind that was the little tenant house on the trailer; and behind that, hitched to the trailer by a short rope, wobbled Imogene looking as if she would be happy to kick anybody who would oblige by coming within range. Behind Imogene, attached to the trailer by a longer rope, stumbled Mark, with Nero bumping his heels skittishly. Nobody ever saw a more real parade.

If there could be any criticism, Fan felt, it was Nero's way with the ditches. "Go easy when you pull out over that deep ditch into the road, Jim," she called across the trailer and tractor. "Nero hasn't got any back, you know, and you could jounce Eddy clear up into the tree."

"Eddy shouldn't have insisted on riding in that—golly, was that a whack," groaned George, whose eyes were fixed in the other direction. "Nero just slam-banged against that old butternut enough to—hey, he did, he did knock half of it right down onto Eddy. Did you see that big black branch or something, Fan?"

Fan flicked about in plenty of time to see it. "But I don't think it was a branch, George," she said. "I wonder why Eddy doesn't kick it out if it was."

3. Braeside

GARDENS can be pretty dull affairs if they are nothing more than petunias, leeks, cabbages, caterpillars, beetles and worms, with hedges everywhere that sprout anew and have to be trimmed after every shower. There is nothing dull about the Braeside gardens, however. They are all different and they are as full of stories as a book.

For instance, there is the first garden on the corner of the County Road and Braeside, across from the store. Captain Todd lives there and he grows shamrock in a thick green patch, ivy in a delicate tangle of vine, and thorn bushes in the four corners. His stories have to do with the shamrock that came from his grandmother's garden in the old country, and the ivy that curtained her low window in the tiny cottage at Bandon, and he'll tell you that his thorn bushes are sprung from the same cruel growth that caught and tore his pants off every time his grandmother wailed that the pig was loose again and what was he, Timmy Todd, going to do about it.

And Mrs. Penny Mold who lives next door has a border of white roses on either side of the front walk. They are tiny white baby roses that need a great deal of trimming to keep them forever in bloom, but Mrs. Mold doesn't mind the work. Only it is hard for her to tell the story of the roses without drying her eyes over and over again on her apron. "You see," she says, "they all came from a garden that my sister Delia planted when we were children living in Cliffton Center. My little sister Delia. She loved these baby roses better than any flowers in the garden and so I keep them to remember her by." And then Mrs. Mold will stop to dry her eyes before going on. "I have the roses," she will continue, "but where is my dear little sister? She crossed the ocean to be wed and to make a new home near the cliffs of Dover, and I've heard no word from her since the terrible war began over there." And then Mrs. Mold will stop to dry her eyes again. For that is the end of her story. There is nothing more she can tell about the sweet little white baby roses.

But next to her lives Mr. Liggard. And if that isn't a story garden! It bristles with sticks or stakes and the sticks and stakes, beyond question, are more interesting than the petunias or zinnias. One stake, the one that holds up a branch of the flowering cherry bush, is made from an elm branch under which George Washington once stood with a few ragged soldiers of the first American army. And one is made from an old, old olive tree that once stood in an enclosed garden near Bethlehem and wore silly little chimes of silver bells on its gnarled boughs. And one stake is made of apple wood from the tree that grew beside the woodshed where Mr. Liggard was born; he has lots of wonderful stories to tell of this stake and of the playhouse he built among the pink and white apple blossoms and of the family of black squirrels that took it over for their own.

Mr. Moom lives just beyond the Liggards in the last house on that side of the street. I suppose there are flowers and stakes and everything in Mr. Moom's garden that anybody else in Braeside has but nobody passing along the street from the County Road to the dock would notice them. The hedge is so important.

Once upon a time Mr. Moom made a tour through distant countries and he found himself, one day, in a castle garden where all the shrubbery had been clipped to look like unicorns and fauns, lions and pagodas. But it was a yew peacock that surprised him most of all. Mr. Moom came back to Braeside determined to have a green peacock growing on his hedge beside the front gate; but when he was all ready to begin, shears in hand, he realized that he didn't know much about a peacock, really. He needed a model, and the only fowls roaming around the north country were turkeys and chickens. And there was something about a turkey's face that he thought would be pretty tiresome to live with, day after day. So Mr. Moom bought the biggest cock in the Cliffton Center market, and clipped its image, with wings widespread as if it was about to fly into the sky (which it tried to do enough times, goodness knows), on his front hedge. Braeside thought he had gone crazy until he showed Captain Todd and Mrs. Mold, the Liggards and Miss Tissy across the way, Mr. Hooke who lived next to her, and Mrs. Witchit who lived between the Hookes and the store on the corner, photographs of the castle garden with green unicorns, fauns, lions, pagodas, and peacocks all over the place. All they could say then was that a thing like that would be too much work for them.

And it was a lot of work. Every shower brought new growth and changed the Cock's contours amazingly. Mr. Moom was continually clipping at it. Of course he had to be careful to leave always a small amount of new fuzzy green (the Cock would have looked like simply nothing at all if he had sheared it back to bare twigs, each time), and so with the years the Cock grew bigger and bigger.

Now Mr. Moom has to stand on a ladder to clip it and the street in front of his gate is cluttered with heaps of greenstuff. He was just about to climb the stepladder, shears in hand, at the exact moment of the little tenant house's departure from its hiding place among the snowberry bushes and the wild grape vines when the tractor thudded and bumped across the ditch, and Nero whammed against the butternut tree. Mr. Moom, far away, bent double to steady himself on the stepladder.

"My goodness," he cried, "what in the world made such a jarring as that? I actually toppled!"

Miss Tissy couldn't tell him. She had been standing out in her garden rubbing catnip leaves between her thin palms because, as she always said, the smell of catnip carried far and wide and that was the only thing that would bring Oliver home from his roamings, sometimes. Sometimes it wouldn't. Sometimes Oliver was having too much fun elsewhere.

"I felt it, I felt it in my feet," she told Mr. Moom. "But don't go blaming my cat for it; he hasn't been home since daybreak. The way you folks blame poor Oliver for everything that happens along this—mercy me, there it goes again. Do you think it can be gunfire at Pine Camp?"

Mr. Moom didn't wait to consider gunfire at Pine Camp. He got down off the ladder and touched ground just as Mr. Liggard popped through his gate waving a link of sausages on a long-handled fork.

"Just starting to fry 'em," he roared. "The stove lids danced and a bowl dropped off the sink shelf. Do you think it could be an earthquake, Moom? There used to be earthquakes in this St. Lawrence section, you know. I can show you pot holes right over on Welles Island where the lid blew off."

"When?" asked Mr. Moom coldly.

"Oh-h, in very early times."

"I should think so. Very early, indeed. Here comes Mr. Hooke. I wonder if he felt the rumble and thudding."

Mr. Hooke had felt it, no doubt about that. "I was transplanting leeks down in the back garden, back of the scarecrow," he said, "and the dibber kicked right out of my fist. They must have set off a right smart blast on that new road they're making across the border. Dynamiting through solid rock in some places."

"But it wasn't in that direction," cried Mrs. Witchit and Mr. Mold, hurrying into Braeside and joining Mr. Liggard, Mr. Moom, Miss Tissy, and Mr. Hooke. "It was off toward The Center," added Mr. Mold. "I wonder where Captain Todd is. All the rest of us are out here in the street, we heard it, it seems funny that——"

And then they saw Captain Todd come out of his garden at the corner of Braeside and the County Road. And they heard him shout that if they wanted to see a chimney traveling from Cliffton Center to Riverhead they'd better lose no more time gossiping down at that end of the street. As for himself, he was going to sit on the store steps.

Well, they all sat on the store steps. And pretty soon they saw the chimney with a bit of roof under it nearing the clump of white birch trees at the bend in the road, and there was smoke coming out of the chimney and the smell of hot johnnycake coming out of some place under the roof.

"There must be a whole house traveling along the County Road," said Mrs. Witchit. "Did you ever!"

"It's Mr. Watson's little tenant house, on a trailer," said Mr. Hanley, the storekeeper, climbing up on a chair so that he could see above all their heads. "His tractor is pulling it."

"Tractor." Mr. Moom was out of patience with himself for not thinking of that before. "No wonder the earth thudded and jarred under our feet. That explains everything."

"It doesn't explain those animals on behind there," squeaked Miss Tissy suddenly. "My soul and body, I should say nothing could explain them. Or that—what is that green cart with a—with something painted on it?"

"Don't look, Tissy," grinned Mrs. Witchit. "The man on that cart has lost some of his paint. My guess is that Bandlo's Circus is moving to Riverhead. Although how they got Watson's little tenant house, and why they want it, beats me. For the love of mercy, that's no circus, look at those children. The trailer is boiling over with golden-headed children."

The shocked silence was so complete on the store steps that everybody heard Mr. Watson quite distinctly when he stood up in his car and shouted to Jim in the tractor behind. "Take it easy around the corner, Jim. Here we are."

Here we are!

Why, "here we are" could have but one meaning. This muddle of house, children, animals and oddments was coming into Braeside with the idea of remaining there. Mr. Liggard removed the sausages from his fork absent-mindedly and hooked a perfectly clean linen handkerchief between the tines in their stead. Miss Tissy leaned against the store door and added her piping to the hubbub.

"You can't move that mess of—that mess of—all those——"

"Buckles," grinned Mr. Watson happily. He wasn't worried over that outcry any more. This was his house and that was his land down at the end of the street. "Yes, ma'am, you just bet you I can move 'all those Buckles' right down into Braeside between you and the river. But how you knew who they are beats me."

"Their golden heads, and they are nothing but midgets, and they'll be all over the place. We can't have children tearing up our gardens, Mr. Watson. We don't want children in Braeside!"

"Children and crows," roared Mr. Hooke. "Between the two we won't have a leek left in the place."

"I suppose," cried Mr. Moom, "that you have the vacant lot across the way from my place in mind, Watson. Braeside will buy it. Name your price and we'll close the deal right here and now." Of course Mr. Watson had had that very lot in mind, but he laughed at the idea of a deal. "That lot is priceless, Moom. It's not for sale," he chuckled.

Mr. Moom turned away and collided with Mr. Liggard without realizing it. Together they stepped into the road and walked to the end of the trailer. "Look at those animals out back there," begged Mr. Liggard. "What kind of an outfit is that for a respectable neighborhood? A houseful of kids and a horse that's like nothing——"

He never finished the sentence. He never knew what happened, really. But Mr. Moom did, much too late. Out of the corner of his eye he saw that all the golden heads weren't inside the little tenant house on the trailer. There was at least one more. It reared for an instant behind the pink and white man that was painted on the little green cart and a shrill voice from inside called out three times, "Maggie! *Maggie!* Maggie!"

That was when it happened. Bandlo's horse sneezed. He sneezed magnificently. He sneezed a sneeze that was to end all sneezes and the draft of it caught Mr. Moom and Mr. Liggard amidships and no two balloon bottles ever did a better disappearing act in any circus tent. Mr. Moom clutched Mr. Liggard and they rolled over together twice in the dust of the County Road, coming up under the rear end of the trailer with Mr. Liggard's handkerchief blown squarely against the indignant Imogene's face.

Mr. Liggard retrieved his property, tucked it into his pocket, felt the sausages and twined them once more around the tines of the long-handled fork. "Gad!" he said.

He was preparing to say more but just then a dot of a lad, looking like a dandelion blossom on an exceedingly short stalk, dropped out of the back door of the little tenant house and, bracing himself, looked down over the rear of the trailer.

"Is this Bandlo's magician, Eddy?" he cried. "This man with the fork?"

"No. Neither of them are. They're too fat."

"One of them is," the dot of a lad on the trailer insisted. "He might be a new one that you didn't see, but he's a magician, all right. He waved a handkerchief and sausages came right out of his pants. If we only had a big hat, now, maybe he could make bunnies come out of it."

"Horace, lovey," Mrs. Buckle came to the door of the little tenant house and beckoned, "come back inside. And you, Fan," she added over her shoulder, "go to the front door and call over the tractor to Mr. Watson that I want to see him back here."

When he came, she said quite distinctly enough for any Braeside listener to understand, "I don't think we want to move in onto your vacant lot, Mark."

"Not move in on—why, Bessie, I don't know what I can do about it, now. I simply must go to Gananoque tomorrow."

"Of course you must, deary. Who owns all this pasture-land along the road across from the store?"

"I do. All the way up to the pine woods above the rocks. And the swale just ahead, if you must know."

"Well, good. That makes everything just lovely. The Buckles won't be annoying anybody if they keep to this side of the road. So have Jim pull us ahead that far and shove us over among the elderberry bushes; kind of switch us around so our back door opens toward the pastures instead of toward this street, this Braeside."

"But, Bessie, it's boggy in that swale."

"Swales generally are dampish, deary." Mrs. Buckle's chuckle was again as merry as a redwing's. "But it'll only be for a day and we won't mind. We'll be high and dry on the trailer; you can leave us on the trailer, can't you, Mark?

And have the boys take the tractor back to the farm?"

"Yes, I could do that. But——"

"We'll have no buts about it, Mark, if you please. I see a well over by the store; we can get water there, and I suppose they'll help us out with whatever else we may need at the store if we pay them for service. Goodness knows, the Buckle children are willing enough to neighbor with anybody, but they know also that it takes two for a bargain like that—one who *wants* a neighbor as well as one who wants to be neighborly. So they'll wait until they are invited before they cross roads or push through gates. Tell Jim to pull us along opposite that house where the thorn bushes are!"

"Todd!" Mr. Watson lifted his voice sharply. "Is it going to fluster you too much to have my foreman's family across the road from you for a day or so? Let's hear all the complaints now. You haven't said a word yet."

Captain Todd didn't say a word then, either. He grinned, found a match in his blouse pocket, scratched it, and kindled a smudge in his old black pipe. His face seemed to fade away behind the tobacco clouds, but Fan was almost sure that she saw him wink at her before it was finally eclipsed. It was a strange gesture for a Braeside dweller, she thought. She climbed into the kitchen, intending to cross the room and peek out of the window where she would be nearer him, but George stopped her on the sill.

"That wasn't a branch that fell out of the butternut

tree on Eddy," he gasped. Fan couldn't believe that
George was so stupid.

"Of course it wasn't," she snapped. "It was Vaughn.
What about him?"

"He just fizzed up out of Nero, and Eddy tried to hold
him in."

"Eddy did? Eddy tried to hold Vaughn in? You don't
mean *in* do you, George?" It was hard for Fan to credit
that part of the story.

She turned back to the opened doorway to see for herself, just in time to hear the wail that blew across the
County Road from the store steps. It was Miss Tissy
again, Fan knew, from the ear-piercing quality of the outcry. "Oliver," piped Miss Tissy. "Oliver Binns. You come
right straight away from those folks this minute. Dear
heavens, where Oliver won't go."

Two by two, the Braeside folks turned homeward, each
in a higher dudgeon than his neighbor, if such a thing
were possible. Mr. Moom and Mr. Liggard dusted each

other's coat sleeves as they trudged along and Miss Tissy blew down Braeside in little gusts of hopping, thinking she had Oliver under her clutching fingers at last and finding that she hadn't.

Only Captain Todd crossed the County Road alone, and in a good humor. He could be heard laughing to himself long after he had passed between the thorn bushes and closed the side door under the ivy vine.

The Buckles forgot them almost at once. Other and more interesting matters caught and held their attention. Jim started up the tractor and, under Mrs. Buckle's direction, he and Fred and Chuck nudged the little tenant house off the side of the road into the edge of the swale and left it there high and dry on the trailer among the elderberry bushes. They took the tractor back to the farm after that, and Mr. Watson and Abijah Buckle went with them, in the car. And so the golden heads were alone again in the queer little house for the second night after giving up their own dear old farm to the army for an airfield.

"There's a difference, though," said Fan cheerily, flitting into the other room for a glance behind the screen in the corner. "We know now where we're going to sleep, and as soon as we shut the doors—hey-y-y, Mother, where are the doors?" she demanded sharply.

"Doors, lovey?"

Fan dropped through the opened doorway of the bedroom, ran around the trailer, and prepared to climb in through the opened doorway of the kitchen. "They're gone," she shrilled. "Both of them, this time."

"Nonsense, deary." Mrs. Buckle looked outside and saw Eddy. "See if Jim left the doors down there anywhere, Eddy," she said.

"He didn't." Eddy knew all about that without looking. "He left both doors and the steps back under the butternut tree, I bet you. And how am I going to get up there?"

"Can't you catch onto something and sort of swing up, deary?"

"I tried that. I'm too little."

"Go over to the store before it closes, Eddy," said Charles, pushing past his mother to drop out of the kitchen onto the trailer. "Ask Mr. Hanley for two empty orange boxes, or something strong. Slap one down there where the bog is driest, and hand the other up here; we'll need it on the trailer so Mother can get in and out of the kitchen."

"Can he get us some doors, too?" asked Fan.

"We won't mind being without doors for just one night, sweety," Mrs. Buckle comforted. "Nobody missed the kitchen door last night."

"But it was just chipmunks, then. Now it could be all those nosy Braeside folks prowling."

"There's nobody in Braeside curious enough about us to prowl and wade and slosh through that swale, Fan. And we won't be curious about them, deary. There's little

Horace with his nose flat against the kitchen window.
Hop down off the stool, son."

"You can see right down through Braeside to the
dock," said Horace, clinging to his perch. "From here,
you can see every single house and the river down there
and all the gardens."

"And that's a good deal more than we care to see,
lovey." Mrs. Buckle swept Horace from the stool, set the
red geranium on the sink shelf, and pulled the shade, shutting the Buckles completely off from all the doings on
the County Road or in Braeside. "Is that Eddy calling,
Delia?"

"Yes'm. He's back, but he hasn't got any boxes. Just a
bag."

The family surged toward the opened doorway. Every
one of them could see by his glowing cheeks and shining
eyes that Eddy had found kindness where he least expected it. "Golly, Mother," he cried, "Mr. Hanley isn't
half bad, do you know it? He said that he didn't blame
Mark at all for blowing Mr. Moom down. He said that
he had wanted to do the same thing himself often, and
he said if I'd come back in the morning he'd give
me——"

"Where are the boxes?" Charles interrupted impatiently.

"On the store steps. I'm going right back after them.
But first I wanted to give Mark this." Eddy waved the

bag proudly. "Oats and stuff for Mark's supper," he explained. "Mr. Hanley gave them to me."

"Law me, what's he going to give you in the morning?" asked Fan.

"Slats."

"Slats." The Buckles, one and all, waited in silence for a clearer interpretation of Mr. Hanley's friendliness.

George was the first to recover. "You don't mean—er—slats, do you?" he asked hoarsely.

"Sure I do. To make a back for Nero, so I won't jounce out. Mr. Hanley said I could hurt myself that way."

"What does he care? He doesn't like children."

"Yes, he does. Some kinds. When he knows them. He's getting to know me."

"He didn't want us to move into Braeside. The fuss they all made when——"

"Not Mr. Hanley. He didn't. There's a crack in Nero's pink nightgown and I was peeking through it when all the ruckus was going on, and two of the folks didn't howl once about bringing us down the street onto Mr. Watson's vacant lot."

"Two?" asked Fan. "Who was the other one?"

"The old man with the pipe. The one who lives across the County Road in the corner house. Captain Todd."

4. Make It a Written Invitation!

B ANG, bang, bang!
Captain Todd opened his door upon a fog that hung in shreds and tatters of thick whiteness, upon a garden pearled with dew. "Wet," he said, "and those tomtits banging away in the swale ever since daybreak. I wonder what they are up to."

He put on his cap, the one that said THE MOLLY in big gold letters all around the band, and stepped briskly along the garden path; he opened the gate and scuffed out into the piles of hedge clippings that lined Braeside. Almost on the instant a ragged sheet of fog broke from the rest and blew across the river leaving a patch of clear blue sky. More fog broke away, blew away.

"Wind's in the west, fish bite best," said Captain Todd, approving the day. "It'll be fine on the water by noon. What's to prevent me from having a fried bass for my supper?"

Bang, bang, bang!

Captain Todd turned his back on the river, faced the County Road, and grinned to himself as he caught a flicker of something pink and something blue. He lifted his cap, and nobody could say that he didn't beckon with it. "It was a good try, anyway," he chuckled, turning about to face the river once more. "If they're as smart as they look——"

"Ssssss-sssssss-sst!"

Captain Todd could have made a better jump if it hadn't been for the small arms around his knobby old knees. A huge dandelion blossom appeared to have sprouted from both pockets of his dungarees, but when he plunged a fist into each fuzzy bloom, turning first one golden ball and then the other upward, he saw his mistake.

"Call me a pink-nosed mullingong if these here objects aren't children," he huffed and puffed.

The twins dissolved in a froth of giggles. "Of course we are children, what did you think?" asked George as soon as he could speak.

"Rattlers, that was my firm opinion, mate," Captain Todd assured him solemnly. "Hissing, sissing snakes aslithering through the heaps of greenstuffs to spike a pore old fisherman in the heel. It's a mercy I didn't leap the dock an' end up in the river."

"With Fan and me holding you down? Don't be silly, you couldn't." Whatever others might think, George, it was evident, considered himself no cock-sparrow. "Not after we grabbed you, you couldn't move. Of course, if you had seen us creeping along under the hedge——"

"Creeping along under the—so that's how you got here, eh?"

"Sure. Didn't you really see us when we dashed across the road?"

"I was watching the fog, like as not."

"No. It was right after you invited us to come and see you."

"I? I invited you? Get out." Captain Todd wiped a grin from his lips with the back of his hand. "Such an idea."

Fan loosed his knobby old knee and her small face darkened. It was the beginning of a blush and Captain Todd was instantly ashamed of himself for causing it. "Didn't you really invite us across the road, sir?" she asked. "Eddy didn't like the way the folks on your street acted last night about us and he said—well, Eddy's kind of proud and he looks after us and he said for us to watch out and not cross the road unless we were really invited. And the trouble we went to, creeping under the hedge and everything, so nobody else would see us, only you. 'Cause you beckoned to us with your cap."

Captain Todd was more ashamed of himself than ever. So ashamed that he, too, almost blushed, and that was something he had never done yet. But then he had never been a bitter disappointment to a pink and a blue fairy before this, either. The sooner he made amends, he felt, the better. He pulled his old black pipe out of his blouse pocket, smacked it against his palm, filled it with tobacco, and kindled himself a smudge to hide behind while he was thinking. He had a brilliant thought almost at once.

"Here now," he said briskly. "Don't you go to jumping at no conclusions, mate. Of course I was beckoning you across the road. Why, sartinly."

Fan brightened and took a fresh hold on the oil-stained dungarees. "To see your pretty garden?" she asked.

"Better than that. I was just planning a fried bass supper for tonight. How'd you kids like to go along, seeing you've got nothing else to do?"

"To get us a fish, too? Boy-y-y!" Fan started to spin on her toes, remembered where she was, and clung closer to the protection of the captain's knobby old knees. "Jim brought us a whole lot of bass last week—ummmmm!" she chuckled. "The best things I like in all the world are pink things, and fish; do you buy your bass over in Mr. Hanley's store, sir?"

"Buy? Buy bass? Why, you can't buy bass along this river, mate. It's against the law. You have to go out and catch 'em yourself."

"Go out where?" asked George. "On the river?"

"It's a good idea. Personally, I prefer Lily Bay."

"Out on the river in a boat, sir?"

"Well, I wouldn't advise traveling about that water in any other way, mate. Say, haven't you two ever been fishing before?"

"We never have."

"Well, well, well!"

"And we can't go now without an invitation," said Fan, tugging at the captain's knee impatiently. "I don't mean just asking us. Eddy wouldn't be satisfied with that. You'd better make it a written invitation."

"A written invitation?" Captain Todd took his pipe out of his mouth and puffed on nothing but foggy morning air for two full minutes, he was so surprised. "Why, that's a real job, mates," he grumbled. "I'm not the writing type. Writing takes paper, and pens, and——"

Fan dropped to her hands and toes and pulled a sheet of soiled paper from the pile of hedge clippings beside the gate. It was a notice of the Cliffton Center Flower Show to be held during the coming week and part of it was far too stained and crumpled to be of any use. She tore that part away and smoothed the rest against the gatepost. "Here you are, sir,—paper," she said. "And George always has a crayon in his pocket. You could print it, if it would be easier than writing for you."

Captain Todd never felt dizzier. "But what shall I say, mates?" he quavered.

Bang, bang, BANG!

"Oh my goodness, hurry, George." Fan all but shook George out of his own blouse, searching for the crayon. "Did you hear that, sir?" she asked.

"I've been hearing banging around here ever since daybreak."

"But not like that. Not with that old buster bang on the end. When Eddy bangs twice and then a real old slambang that means, 'Where are you, F. and G.? Mind your step!' It really means business, sir. Why do you have to have so many pockets, George? If I had so many I'd keep a crayon in each one."

"Get out. I know where it is." George was annoyed by so much assistance. "It's under the worm——"

Fan got out with a leap and a yelp. Captain Todd steadied her against his knee. "You didn't tell me yet about that other banging," he hinted. "You folks building an addition onto Watson's house?"

"Mercy no! Eddy's putting a back on Nero."

"Nero? Another Buckle?"

"Yes, sir. I guess he's got to be if Eddy says so. But I'm awf'ly ashamed about it, sir. We never had a fat man in a pink nightgown in our family before."

"Aw, he'll be all right." George had the crayon and felt able once more to deal with outside matters. "Eddy said when he got around to it he'd fix him up all right. Maybe he'll paint the nightgown green like the rest of the cart."

"And leave that fat man foaming right up out of nothing—I mean with nothing around him?"

Captain Todd dipped into the discussion. "The horse is lean enough," he said. "Must be Nero ate the cream of all the family meals."

"Well, he isn't so lean now." Fan's eyes widened as she thought of the change in Mark. "You ought to see him just since yesterday, sir. Mother says we imagine it, but a horse couldn't eat what Mark does and not swell out somewhere. He'll slurr-rr-r-uppp up a bucket of stuff before you can say, 'God bless this meal.' "

"He's Eddy's Vic." George defended Mark's appetite boldly. "He's got to get his strength back so as to help Eddy win the war. You know about the war, don't you, sir?"

"Yup. Even in Braeside we know about that. Everybody's as mad as a wet hen over it."

"Mad? About the war? Why are they?"

"Oh-h, Mr. Mold, he lives in that house next to me, Mold can't get a new-fangled hedge clipper he had his heart set on before the government stopped their make; and Liggard, down in the next house beyond Mold's, he was all packed up for a trip to furrin parts when poof, no ships. And Moom can't buy a thick steak for his dinner; and what Miss Binns has to say about no more canned salmon isn't delicate."

"Can't she eat bass?"

"Oliver prefers salmon."

"Oliver? That big black——"

Bang, bang, BANG-G!

Fan leaped for the crayon and jammed it into Captain Todd's fist. "Quick," she panted. "Eddy won't wait much after a bang like that. Just say that F. and G., that's Fan and George, you know, are invited by——"

"Captain Todd at your service," the captain concluded the introductions.

The twins nodded politely, and centered their interest on the torn scrap of paper while the crayon moved rapidly from top to bottom.

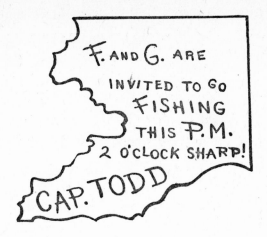

"There," said George when the last letter was printed on the document. "Let's see what Eddy has to say to that. Step on it, Fan."

The Buckles vanished into the fog-like wisps of pink and blue vapor and Captain Todd returned to his own kitchen door. "Fried bass for supper tonight," he told himself in high spirits. "And a couple of nice kids to take fishing. Well, well, well!"

Two hours later he was out on the garden path, fishing gear in hand. Poles, lines, reels, a tin box of plugs, a gaff, a landing net. Mr. Mold opened his shop door and whistled.

"Going fishing, Todd?" he asked.

"What do you think?"

"I think it's a good idea! If I didn't have some garden

work to do I'd go with you. My nerves are all shot to pieces listening to that bang, bang, banging ever since before daybreak. If you'd care to wait for half an hour, maybe I could finish up what I planned to do and go with you."

"Sorry," roared Captain Todd, quickening his step. "Can't wait today." He stepped outside the gate into Braeside.

"Ssssss-sśs-ss-sst!"

"Dod blast it all, rattlers agin," he growled, spanking a heap of hedge clippings with his landing net. "The place is full of 'em."

The pile of greenstuffs heaved convulsively and a pink tag, like a hollyhock petal, showed for an instant. "Ouch," giggled Fan. "Who do you think you're hitting? And you didn't tell the truth, 'cause you aren't sorry that that man isn't coming with us."

Captain Todd dropped his landing net experimentally on a second heap of clippings and a blue arm seized hold upon it. "That's a very good idea, sir," George whispered hoarsely. "Keep pretending you're dropping this and the rest of your stuff all over the place and that will give Fan an' me time to crawl along under the hedges and the greenstuff without being noticed. Eddy said that nobody else in Braeside was to see us, only you. So, if you just pretend to fumble with your tennis racket the folks will say, 'Poor old man, poor old man.' "

"Here now!"

"Drop something, quick. I want to skitter over that bare spot. It was a lucky thing you gave us a written invitation, sir. Eddy wouldn't have believed us without it. He read it over and over, and then he turned it over on the other side and read the printing, and then he put it in his pocket and said, 'Okay.' " •

"He must have liked it," Fan added, " 'cause he kept it for himself. He's sitting on the trailer where he can look right straight down Braeside to the dock and if he sees us, he said, other folks could, too. So we've got to keep under cover. These trash heaps certainly come in handy when you haven't been invited to a place, don't they, sir?"

"Is that your boat?" asked George, after one quick peep ahead.

"That's THE MOLLY, mates. The best old fishing dory on the river."

"Then give him the can, George. And watch that cover so it doesn't fall off."

"Can?" Captain Todd accepted a coffee can and shook it curiously.

"You don't need·to do that," Fan warned. "They're healthy, all right. Boy-y-y-y, you ought to see them kick. Eddy said if we were going fishing with you we'd have to provide part of the entertainment, so he went out into the swale while we were eating and got a whole can of hop-toads. Though what he got that goshawful worm for, I'll never know," she added bitterly. And then, with a sharp cry, she warned, "Duck, George, duck!"

George ducked. Almost, it might be imagined, Captain Todd ducked with him. "Golly," he exclaimed. "What's wrong, mate?"

"A man's watching us."

"A man? Where?"

"Across the street. A Preacher Man, an' he's dancing like sixty."

George heaved among his evergreens and stared. "It's the Reverend Carr from Cliffton Center," he gasped, "and he's got his angels with him. They're flying all around his hat."

"Where?" demanded Fan, throwing off her hedge blanket and standing forth in the open regardless of consequences. "Where did you see an angel, George?"

Bang!

"Oh my goodness!" Fan fell on her face and drew a coat of green about her head and shoulders. "If you hadn't have stood right in front of me, Eddy would have seen me, sir, and then we would have had to go back to the swale," she said. "One bang means he almost did, but he wasn't sure, but watch your step, F. and G. Where is the angel, George?"

"One is on the Reverend Carr's hat now. It came right down out of the sun and lit there."

Captain Todd's laughter shocked the twins. "Angels," he sputtered as soon as he could catch his breath. "Angels, oh my! No angels, mates. That's the Reverend's high black topper, right enough, my lad. Or was, until his last call in Braeside. He came to see Miss Tissy and Oliver clawed his leg. Both of them went down together in a mud puddle. The Reverend had to go home bareheaded and Miss Tissy gave what was left of the topper to Mr. Hooke."

"What did he want it for?" Fan wanted to know.

"For his scarecrow. That's your dancing gentleman across the street, George. Mr. Hooke has quite a time keeping the old boy in headgear, and you can't deny a Reverend's hat does give quite a blessed look to the leeks and onions. It was the first kind word Mr. Hooke was ever heard to speak about Oliver Binns, when he gave him credit for the new lid. Oliver is quite a digging cat, you know. But it won't last long. That hat will go the way of all the rest."

"What way?" asked George.

"Oh-h, Oliver's. Oliver found a field mouse under an old alpine hat that Mr. Moom donated, once, and there's a cat that never forgets. Just as soon as he notices a new hat on the scarecrow he settles right down to the business of ripping it apart. Digging and ripping, that's Oliver Binns."

"That isn't Oliver flying around the hat now, though."

"Oh no. Oliver doesn't do all the ripping along this river. The crows from One-Tree Island like the scarecrow's hats, too."

"George, duck!" warned Fan fiercely.

"What, again?" George's heap of green was motionless. "Is it flying?"

"Yes. Right over your head."

"Puff! Who cares for an old crow."

"It isn't a crow, George. It's green."

"Green?" George humped on his hands and knees and his golden head blossomed in full view of anybody who might be watching Braeside. Captain Todd moved in front of it and spread his dungarees for a shield. "Gosh, it's a cock," he piped. "A cock as big as Mark. I wish Katy an' Lulu could see him once. Maybe they wouldn't think they were so much-a-much, then. Can he ever get off that hedge, Captain Todd?"

"Of course he can't. He's cut out of the evergreen."

"Who cut him?"

"Mr. Moom."

"Boy-y-y!" Fan jostled her twin into mindfulness of where they were. "Let's get away from here," she advised. "He's the man that Mark sneezed upside down. How do we get down where your boat is, sir?"

Captain Todd paused only long enough to light his pipe and gather up his fishing gear. "We dash across the street and cut down through the vacant lot, over the bank to my dock," he directed. "Hug up close to me while we cross the street and nobody'll see you. After that you can stand up and walk like men. Nobody can possibly spot such titmice as you once we start to wade through the weeds the other side of Miss Tissy's fence."

"Vacant lot?" asked Fan. "Where?" And then, after only one peep and no more, she sat flat on her pink sunsuit and forgot all about THE MOLLY bumping against the dock under the bank. "Is that Mr. Watson's vacant lot, where he was going to move us?" she wanted to know.

"That's the place."

"Well, sir, what old meanies the Braeside folks are," she said bitterly, and didn't care who might be listening. "Just look at that vacant lot, George, all over white and gold and blue and pink. And smell of it. And the best thing I like in all the world is pink."

Mr. Watson's lot was, indeed, all over white and gold and blue and pink. It was smothered in white daisies, golden buttercups, purple vetch, and rosy dogbane. And the breath of the dogbane was as heavy and sweet as the rare arbutus. And beyond, clear across to the haze that meant Canadian shore, was the mighty width of the blue, blue St. Lawrence River rolling onward to the sea.

"Boy-y-y!" gasped George. "Look at the big boat away out there."

"On its way to England, lad. Salute a brave ship and a gallant crew."

The twins saluted solemnly. And after that they lost no time in crossing the street and sliding down the bank to the dock where THE MOLLY was moored. Captain Todd lifted them aboard the bobbing old dory and Fan promptly seated herself on a plank in the bow with her feet crossed under her. George perched on a box near the captain's knee. They had nothing to say until THE MOLLY nosed into the carpeting green pads of Lily Bay and Captain Todd threw out his anchor.

Then Fan wanted to know what else he was going to throw out, and looked meaningly at the coffee can.

"Why, a line or two, I expect, after I have wetted them up," Captain Todd replied cheerfully. "Three, if you want to catch a bass with the mate and me," he added, winking at George.

"I don't want the cover off that can, you know," she warned sharply.

"You don't want the cover—— How do you think we're going to feed the fish, then?"

"Throw out the can and let 'em open it themselves."

Captain Todd was astonished beyond words. He remembered almost at once that the twins had not been fishing before, but he supposed that some facts were just naturally born into children. This was bad. "We don't feed fish by handing 'em a plate and maybe a spoon and fork," he explained with a grin. "We dip into the can, and get out a hoptoad, and stick it on a hook, like this, and——"

"Oh, my gosh!"

"——and whang it out as far as the line will go, like this," Captain Todd continued with his lesson, unmoved. "Then we reel it in slow and steady, slow and steady, slow and steady."

"The same old hoptoad? You bring that same old jumper right back inside this boat?"

"Unless a bass sees him first. Then he rides back inside the bass."

"What's your tennis racket for? I thought you'd maybe scoop a fish up in it, the way Charles catches butterflies."

"If it's a big fish I'll slip the landing net under him, all right, an' hist him over into the fish box."

"That thing that George is sitting on?"

"That's it."

"Well, law me. You'd let George sit right there on top of all the hopping, flopping things you could think of. I don't think that's very nice when you invited us to, well, to have a kind of picnic. We don't have picnics like that at our house. George, you come right over here and sit on the plank with me. I bet you he wouldn't care if there was another goshawful worm in that box." Fan wanted to spin on her toes and buzz like an excited wasp, but of course she couldn't do that in THE MOLLY. All she could do was to pat the plank and wait for George to join her on it.

5. Captain Todd Loses—and Finds—a Fish Supper

GEORGE showed no interest in the plank in the bow of THE MOLLY. Until today George had accepted his twin's orders good-naturedly but now, for the first time in his life, he realized that there was a dividing line between pink sunsuits and blue overalls, and he was shocked at finding himself so close to the wrong side of that line.

Fan was a girl. Fan was afraid of worms and hoptoads, of all things that kicked and flopped and hissed, too. She didn't fret when Charles was kicked by Imogene, or Eddy by Mark, or when little Horace was hissed at by Oliver Binns, because boys weren't expected to be afraid of anything. But she hauled George away from a hoptoad. Why, Fan must think that he was a girl, too. Golly!

George opened the coffee can, removed the goshawfulest worm, and seated himself again upon the fish box with it squirming in his fingers, waiting for Captain Todd's hook. "Here you are, sir," he said. "Let's see what this'll catch." And then to his twin he remarked coldly, "Don't fuss so much, Fan, when you're out with us menfolks.

Play with the lilies, or watch the birds, but hush up. Captain Todd and I are busy."

"Blessed if we aren't," roared the captain proudly. "By gorry, I have got me a mate!" And then he baited a fresh hook for George with one of the healthiest of the hoptoads, and suggested that he keep his line on one side of the dory, while he himself would consider the other side as Todd territory. And so silence and peace settled down over Lily Bay.

Fan couldn't understand it. Where was the fun in slapping the water over and over again with a tired, messy old hoptoad? She flopped about on her plank and lay full length on her pink sunsuit with her face close to the lovely white drifts of lilies.

Suddenly she coiled like a tiny spring and squeaked, "Julia! Captain Todd, our duck's out there on your old river."

George held his hook free of the water and looked where she pointed but could see nothing. "You're crazy," he sniffed. "Julia's in her basket with Katy and Lulu."

"She was, but she isn't now! She's—she's——"

"All right, where is she?"

Fan was puzzled. "She was out there in that empty place between the lilies, an' she popped under the water, an'—there, now you can see her, George."

George was as surprised as anybody could be. "I did see her," he cried. "Before she drowned herself. Dove right down under the water an' now she's gone."

Captain Todd lit his pipe and made another cast. "That isn't your duck, mate," he explained. "That's a hell-diver. Lily Bay's full of 'em. First you'll see one sitting pretty on the waves here and another one yonder, and then they'll dive and no sign of one anywhere. They'll stay under water till you give 'em up for lost, and then up they'll pop where you least expect it."

"It looked just like Julia, sir."

"Sugar and salt look alike, too, but—hey-y, look at that fish, will you. Just nosed against my bait, backed off, and went right under the dory."

"I should think he would run from a worm like that." Fan tilted her nose delicately. "I should think he'd run like sixty."

"Gorr-rr-r-y!" roared the captain, half rising to his feet. "What goes on here?"

"A fish, a fish, I got me a fish!" shrieked George, bracing his small legs and holding onto his pole with all his might.

Far in the distance, the water split and something very lovely rose in the sunlight to curve in a shower of crystal drops before dropping back beneath the water. Captain Todd stared, popeyed. He didn't believe what he had seen, not until the water parted for the second time to allow the curving thing another swift flight through crystal rain. Then he knew.

"Dod blast it, I should say that you have got you a fish," he howled. "You've hooked into the best bass taken out of Lily Bay since—you've hooked into my fish, George.

The one that nosed my bait an'—hey-y, don't give that line any slack, mate. Reel in, keep him comin', keep him comin'; here, give me the rod."

Fan was incensed. "Don't you do it, George," she shrilled. "He said that was our terr'tory; keep him comin', George, keep him comin'.'"

Through a bit of pure luck and not because of any advice ringing about his unheeding ears, George managed to swing the bass inside the dory before he subsided like a pricked balloon. Captain Todd opened the fish box expectantly. Fan reached out with the gaff and slapped it shut. "My goodness, he's just bound to get our fish, George," she cried. "Watch out. Don't put it in that box. Keep it right out where we can see it; put your heel on it. Boy-y, look at that thing jerk."

"He won't jerk much more, mate."

"I don't mean our fish, I mean your stick." Fan pointed with a sliver of a finger. "Something's dragging it right out into the water."

Captain Todd stood up with a roar. "Back, mates," he warned. "I'll need plenty of room to reel this one in. Acts kind of like a muskie to me. You be ready with that gaff when I call for it, Fan, and—— Well, blast my bunkers, if it isn't a punkin seed."

A punkin seed, it seemed, was a fish that could cause a riverman deep chagrin. Particularly when hooked before witnesses. The twins were sorry for their host's embarrassment although they could see no reason for it.

"Of course he isn't fat like mine," said George, comparing the lean, flat object dangling from the captain's finger with what was held firmly beneath his own small heel. "But he's kind of pretty, at that."

Captain Todd sat down and opened his hunting knife.

"What are you going to do, sir?" quavered Fan, drawing her feet up on the plank.

"I'm going to get back my bait, hook, line, plug, and sinker." Captain Todd was forgetting nothing. "The only thing a punkin seed won't swallow is the dory."

"Will he give 'em back?"

"He'll give 'em back or I'll know the reason why. Just you watch and see."

Fan didn't, of course. Not after the first few minutes. "Messy," she decided, and turned her attention to the peculiar habits of hell-divers. "But you could pick up the bits, George," she suggested thoughtfully, "if the captain doesn't want them."

"What do I want 'em for either?" George was offended. "That fish is ruined."

Fan stretched out on her face once more and trailed her fingers in the water. "Sure it is," she agreed. "But Eddy might like it. He bought a sardine for Vaughn this morning. This could save him money. There, I got one!"

Captain Todd was astounded. Also grieved. "You got one?" he boomed, scattering fins, scales, and bits of punkin seed around the dory like hail. "You caught a fish barehanded?"

"Of course not, silly." Fan drew her arm out of the water and dried it delicately on the back of her pink knee. "I'm fishing for lilies, and look at the buster I got." She drew her catch to the plank and beamed upon it pridefully. "I'm going to catch a whole bucketful for Mother and Delia," she announced. "The way they love flowers, lilies will be a comfort to them when we have to move away from where they can peek under the kitchen shade at the Braeside gardens tomorrow."

Captain Todd sat down on the fish box and drew his brows together. "I wish I knew what you were talking about," he complained.

"Why, us. And the window in our kitchen on the trailer, and your nice gardens," she chuckled.

"I got that much. But about moving away tomorrow."

"Well, maybe not tomorrow. But just as soon as Mr. Watson comes for us. After he gets his new family, of course. You knew that Mr. Watson was getting a new family from across the border, didn't you?"

Captain Todd had never known less of anything than he did of this news. "A new family, old Watson?" he marveled. "No."

"Yes, he is. A dozen kids, he said, if the committee wanted to send him that many. English, Dutch, Polish or what have you, he said. He didn't care what they were, just so they were hungry and scared of bombs. And Jim said the farm was big enough to feed a dozen and a half."

"And the mamas, too," added George. "Mr. Watson

thinks it would be nice if some poor mamas came along from over where the war is."

"Boy-y-y!" Fan sighed and patted her lily. "We take care of our Vics, and we earn money for the Chests of Cheer, but I do wish we could have some more family, too."

"That," said Captain Todd, "is what the Buckles need least of anything in the world, I should say. More family. Gorry!"

"But our alphabet's only down as far as N-is-Nero." George resented something in the captain's tone of voice. "We've got a long way to go yet. Hey, Fan, why don't you wish on a lily?"

"Why, that's so, I could." Fan flicked about, facing the fishermen. "You know about wishing on a lily don't you, Captain?"

"Never heard of it."

"Law me, what you have missed. Well, you take a lily like this, and you hold it under your chin, and then you say,

> I make three wishes on a lily,
> One, two, three!
> I kiss the heart, I kiss the petals,
> I pull the stem and set it free!"

"And now she really does, you know," explained George, leaning forward to check the proceedings carefully. "She sets it out on the river, afloat again. Go on, Fan."

"When it comes back 'twill bring my wishes
Three to me!

And now I have to make mine. Or would you rather wish
first?" she asked the old captain politely.

Captain Todd declined hastily. "Can't think of a thing
in the world to wish for," he said, hacking another chunk
out of the punkin seed.

Fan was amazed. "And you without a single child on
your street," she hinted delicately. "Why, there's the
most things to wish for, like helping the poor people over
where the war is, or making folks around you happier, or
—oh, you take a lily home with you and think it over and
I bet you you'll come running back to the river with it to
set it free bearing three perfectly dandy wishes. Like
maybe having a nice little boy or girl in every house in
Braeside, or something like that. Now, I'll make my first
one. Quiet everybody, an' clamp down on that fish,
George, he's flopping again." She buried her dot of a nose
in the lily's golden heart and murmured,

"I kiss you. Please be kind, my dear,
And help the Buckles earn more gold
To fill the Chests of Cheer!

Of course it doesn't have to be gold, you know," she explained hastily. "Dollar bills will do. Now my second wish
is going to be different.

I have to kiss your petals for my second wish today,
Please let the Buckles live in Braeside, never move away!"

George lifted a howl of disappointment. "There, you wasted that one," he cried. "Golly, I thought you were smarter than that. It isn't fair to wish for something that you know you won't get, and you know perfectly well, Fan Buckle, that we've got to move away from Braeside as soon as Mr. Watson comes for us."

"It's kind of nice here."

"Sure it is, but the folks don't like us. Mother says we could never live where we weren't welcomed. The folks won't even look us over, to see if they would maybe like us or not."

"Captain Todd did." Fan smiled upon her host warmly. "Anyway, give it a chance, George, you never can tell what a lily-wish will do. And now I'm going to nip off the blossom and set it afloat."

"That third wish'd better be good," George grumbled. "It's the last one, remember."

"It'll be good, all right. Listen!

And now I break your long green stem, and float you where
　　'tis wet,
Please send us lots more letters for our Buckle alphabet!

There! If those three wishes don't do the trick——"

Bang, bang, BANG!

"Well, my gosh," gasped George. "I didn't know we
could hear Eddy 'way out on the river."

"We could always hear Eddy, I guess, if he wants us to
come home." Fan sighed and gathered the rest of her
dripping lilies to her breast. "Tell THE MOLLY to gaddup,
sir, or whatever you have to say to make her step on it.
Maybe Mr. Watson is back already, and Jim's coming
with the tractor; anyway Eddy says we've got to hurry
back to the swale."

The old dory barely scraped the Braeside dock before
the twins were outside, scrambling up the bank to the
vacant lot. They stopped once, knee deep in daisies, buttercups, vetch and dogbane, to wave farewell, and then
they vanished.

"Dod blast it all, if I don't believe they are fairies," said
Captain Todd to himself, moving along the dock to where
he could watch the length of the street and its piles of
hedge clippings as far as the County Road. "The way they
fade from sight. You'd think that scrap of pin cambric and
those blue overalls—— Here now, what's this all about?
Where's my fish?"

He scuffed a scale and slice of punkin seed aside, but that wasn't the fish he meant. "Why, the little varmints," he growled. "They knew that fish nosed my bait first, I told them so plain. And more than that, the catch always belongs to the boat. By all the river rules, that bass was mine. I let George boast about hauling it in 'cause it tickled the kids so, but when it come to eating time I fully expected——"

And then he heard, in memory, an ecstatic little cry, "Oooo, ummmmmm! The best things I like in all the world are pink things, and fish!"

"Pshaw," said Captain Todd aloud, probably to THE MOLLY this time. "Let 'em have it. Let 'em have an afternoon and a fish supper to remember all the rest of their lives, even if I have lost my fish supper. I'll get me a slab of bacon at the store," he stopped and scowled, "though how I'm going to explain to Bill Hanley that I'm back from Lily Bay with no bass, I don't know. He'll think I'm aging an' losing my grip on river business."

He shambled wearily up Braeside through late afternoon scents of wallflowers, four-o'-clocks, clove pinks, stocks, and—— "Catnip," he growled, opening the side door to his shop. "When Miss Tissy rubs that weed in her hands it tops all other smells around here. Oliver must be roaming again."

He dropped his fishing gear and hurried across the street in order to catch Mr. Hanley before he had locked the store for the night.

"Hold everything, Bill," he shouted. "I need a slab or two of——"

Mr. Hanley was impatient for his own supper table. "All right, what'll it be?" he asked sharply. "A minute more and the last light would have been out."

"Bill," said Captain Todd, "I smell fish."

"You wouldn't have much of a nose if you didn't." Mr. Hanley turned on a light near the front door and stepped aside. "The place reeks with it. By morning everything that isn't in tins will be tainted."

Captain Todd drew near the front door and looked, unbelievingly, upon a flat brown basket that was balanced on Mr. Hanley's own stool in the corner. "Bass," he gasped. "I hope the game warden doesn't hear about this, Bill. You'll find yourself in plenty of misery if it gets about that you have been selling bass in the store."

"I'm not selling bass. Don't be foolish, Todd."

"What's it doing here, then?"

"I know the law, Todd, as well as you do, and I obey it, but that isn't saying I'm not an old soft-head, because I am. I wish Watson would come back from Gananoque and do something about those kids of his."

"Watson? How does he fit into the picture? You don't mean the Buckles, do you?"

"I certainly do." Mr. Hanley reached under the counter and hauling forth a tangle of wilted water lilies and a pile of punkin seed hash wrapped in a scrap of linen added them to the bass on the basket. "When a bunch of golden-headed innocents come into my store with a mess like this and a signboard—you didn't notice the signboard, did you, Todd? Watch out, the paint's wet yet—they fixed the whole thing up in the last ten minutes."

Captain Todd stooped to read while Mr. Hanley explained further.

"When a bunch of golden-headed mites come into my store and ask me to put this on a stool beside the door, what am I going to say to them? It seems they are great war workers, they've washed dishes and weeded onions and I don't know what all where they lived before, but now since they've been in that little tenant house they haven't known how to pick up any business and they are afraid the war's getting way ahead of them. But now the one in the smallest pink sunsuit's got an idea. The best thing she likes in all the world, says she, is fish, so she'll sacrifice her bass supper and turn the money into something she calls the Chests of Cheer. But I told her, over and over again, it was against the law for me to sell bass in the store, so what does the lad called Eddy say? He says for me not to sell it, just to leave it on the basket; and if anybody wants it for supper, they can have it and leave whatever they want to on the basket in pay, for the Chests of Cheer, of course. In that way, he figures, since there's no price tag on it and since it is for charity, oh well, what could I do? I'm not selling it, I haven't had a finger on it. They are kind of nice kids, do you know it, Todd?"

"I do," Captain Todd replied solemnly. "The one in the smallest pink sunsuit, as you call it, is named Fan. You know what her mother said last night about neighbors— hands across the road? Well, it's a fact, Bill. We tried it this afternoon and Fan and George and I like each other fine. I aim to make a few introductions around Braeside later, strictly under cover, you know, if I see the going is too hard for the Buckles. But not too soon. Better let them sell themselves to our folks in their own way. Wrap up the bass, the punkin seed hash, and the lilies, Bill, and tell me what I ought to leave to pay."

"Not me. I'm not selling bass in this store, Todd," said Mr. Hanley sternly, "and don't you ever forget it. A quarter ought to satisfy them, I should think."

"Twenty-five cents? You're crazy, Bill. The wish was for gold, but Fan was willing to compromise on dollar bills.

So here's a dollar for her sacrifice, and here's another dollar for George. George is offering the punkin seed hash, in case you don't know. I'll take the lilies along for good measure. I might like to use one after dark."

"Bless me, if I don't think you are crazy, Captain," said Mr. Hanley. "But don't tell me. The less I know about this deal the better. If any game warden shows up around here I'll refer him to you, and don't think I won't. Here you are, Todd, all wrapped up. Go out the back way, and don't let anybody see you."

Nobody saw Captain Todd go home through the gathering dusk. But that is not to say that nobody smelled him. Oliver Binns, on the prowl about Braeside, leaped suddenly forward and took the short-cut through Mr. Hooke's leeks, over Mrs. Witchit's hedge, across the street, and under Captain Todd's gate. And so reached the captain's side door just in time to have it slammed shut in his face. Oliver yeowl-ll-led. When nothing came of it, Oliver scratched at the door and yeowl-ll-lll-ll-lled longer and louder. He was all set for a third attack when, to his everlasting astonishment, the Todd door opened gently and instead of receiving a pail of water in the face, which had happened more than once, Oliver was summoned to a very nice snack of hashed punkin seed under the lilac bush. If it had been anything else, Oliver would have been cautious about approaching the offering, but he never could resist fish, so he leaped upon it with a fizz and a siss.

And found no unpleasant surprise prepared for him. It was an evening of pure delight, something that Mr. Binns would remember as long as he remembered the field mouse under the alpine hat on the head of Mr. Hooke's scarecrow.

Much later, oh very much later, when it was black dark in fact, the Todd door opened once again, rather slyly this time, and the captain crept forth into the night. He held something droopy in his hand and he headed for the dock with it. If any of the Braeside folks had seen him then they certainly would have said, "Poor old man, poor old man." Some might even have come right out bluntly and asserted that the captain had lost whatever mind he once had. Because Captain Todd was carrying a water lily.

On the dock he lifted the faded lily to his nose, and then he pressed his lips to the petals, and then he snapped the blossom from the stem and tossed the whole thing over into the river. "There, old Lady Luck," he snickered. "Now let's see you make good. Let's see you send this lily back to me with Wish Number Two all fulfilled, nice as can be. Never mind about more gold for the Chests, or more letters for the alphabet. Just concentrate on that Number Two wish an' we'll call it a deal. Golly, what a riverman I could make out of George."

6. The Buckles Have a Holiday

Eddy collected the two dollar bills from the flat brown basket when he went to the store the next morning, Saturday, for the milk. He put them in his pocket in rather a dumpish frame of mind, it seemed to Mr. Hanley.

"Pretty good haul you made there, son," said Mr. Hanley without, however, brightening the sober little face under the golden thatch. "Two bucks ought to be enough for any man's bass."

"It's too much. Fan'll put up a howl about leaving here, now."

"Oh, she'll learn money doesn't come as easy as that around Braeside all the time."

"But this money came, and that was the first of her three wishes. George said she wished on a lily yesterday and the first wish was for some more Chest money. She won't see any reason why, if she got this wish, she won't get the others, and it's the others that she's banking on most of all. She could weed onions, you know, and make the first wish come true all by herself. But she needs heavy help with the other two wishes, and she counts on the lily."

"Maybe she'll get 'em."

"No chance." Eddy picked up his milk pail and was gone.

And the Braeside folks saw nothing of the Buckles all the rest of that day. They were staying about the swale, waiting for Mr. Watson. The twins aired Katy and Lulu until all that the two little chickens wanted was a long, long rest in their covered basket; they bathed Julia until she flew into a rage at the mere sight of the new dishpan, which seemed a pretty good substitute for a brook the first time she dove into it; and they fed Mark. All day long, they fed Mark.

But toward the end of the day, as the evening mist began to roll in from the river, to cross the road and the swale and climb the slanting pastures beyond, making everything silver on gold where the buttercups were and silver on blue where the harebells danced and silver on rose where the dogbane scented the breeze with its arbutus-like breath, by that time even the Buckles had had enough of the swale for a little time. They climbed, one by one, from the orange box to the trailer and from there into the kitchen of the little tenant house and stood in a soggy circle around the kitchen table.

"What you making, Mother?" asked Fan, helping herself to a hard lump of brown sugar.

"Spice cookies, lovey."

"Mr. Watson didn't come for us after all."

"Now, now, deary, don't be impatient. It takes more days than you could hold in one hand, remember, to make a year."

"A year!" Fan was shocked until she saw her mother wink merrily at Delia and then she let out her breath with a relieved puff. "Boy-y-y, you had me scared for a minute," she said. "If we had to wait a year for Mr. Watson—heck, I don't like days when nothing happens."

"Something did happen today," Delia reminded her quickly. "Julia laid an egg."

"No wonder. She got so mad she had to do that or bust."

"And I got twenty-five cents for it." Delia patted her pocket proudly.

"Who took it off the basket?" asked Fan curiously.

"I don't know. But if Julia lays another egg tomorrow, and Monday, and Tuesday, I'll have as much money for the Chests as you got for your fish."

Fan was pained. "Law me, you don't think we'll be perched up here on a trailer until next Tuesday, do you?" she demanded.

"You wished that we'd live in Braeside forever and ever," George reminded her.

"Not on top of this trailer, I didn't." Fan flitted across the room and peeped under the shade that was drawn against the kitchen window. Dots of light were beginning to bud on both sides of Braeside, from the County Road to the dock. "This isn't living in Braeside," she cried sharply.

"Why, we can't even go into Braeside without crawling on our stomachs under trash heaps."

"We can't go anywhere," George agreed with a groan. "Golly, my legs hurt from just standing still on 'em."

Mrs. Buckle stopped beating spice cookies and looked down at the six bored little faces. "Well, sir," she chuckled merrily, "if I wasn't forgetting about how you kids would miss our old place in The Center, the sheds and the wide fields, the brook and the barn and the woodlot. I've felt kind of cramped myself the last few days, and you've been mighty brave and cheery about all this upset. I tell you what we need now, we need a Holiday!"

Six small faces brightened like candles held to a flame. Until Charles blew the light out by reminding them that it would be impossible for them to leave the swale for a Holiday lest Mr. Watson and the tractor arrive while they were away and pull their house off somewhere where they couldn't find it.

"Shucks, the things you think of, deary," laughed Mrs. Buckle, reaching for the cinnamon. "Mr. Watson won't come tomorrow, tomorrow's Sunday. We'll have us a day to remember."

"San'wiches an' everything, in the covered basket?" cried Fan.

"Sure thing, sweety."

"Dump Julia an' Katy an' Lulu out, George," cried Fan, beginning to buzz. "Put 'em somewhere else."

"Where?"

"Oh, anywhere. Put 'em in the big scrub bucket under the sink, they couldn't climb out of that. Where'll we go, Mother, for our Holiday?"

"Why, what's the matter with Aunty Belle's house?"

There were plenty of things, it seemed, the matter with Aunty Belle's house and all six Buckles were willing to name them. "Do you call that a Holiday?" demanded George, gaining the air for the moment. "All of us boys, even little Horace, having to wear neckties!"

"An' I hope you haven't forgotten the last time we were there," Fan carried on with the lament, "when I spilled a drop of gravy on her tablecloth—boy-y-y!"

"It's a long way to Aunty Belle's, Mother!" said Eddy, turning certain angles of the proposed trip over in his mind with increasing suspicion. "An' that covered basket is good and heavy when it's full of picnic stuff. Who's going to carry it, with Father in Gananoque?"

"I was counting on Mark and Nero, lovey."

"Mark hasn't hardly got his strength back yet."

"Oh, fiddlesticks, don't you fret about Mark's strength, the way he's been stuffing himself the last few days. What he needs now is exercise."

"I don't want to go to Aunty Belle's," howled little Horace suddenly, to the surprise of everybody. The Buckles argued their disappointments thoroughly, but they rarely shed tears over them. "I don't want to wear a tight old necktie." He walked under the kitchen table and lunged angrily at a back leg. "I'll tip it over, an' I'll spill the spice cookies an' I'll spill the gravy an' I'll——"

Mrs. Buckle reached under the table and extracted little Horace from his hiding place. She sat down on a stool, took him in her lap, and sponged off his hot face with a damp towel. "Now I'll tell you what I'll do," she promised, as merrily as though all the Buckles were playing the funniest game in the world. "I'll slip the pan of spice cookies into the oven, and then I'll set out a bowl of bread and ice-cold milk for each of us, an' then I'll give a smack on whatever's bare to the last one in bed. An' tomorrow the Holiday'll look better to all of us. We'll get up in the cool of the morning and we'll take our time sauntering along the River Road to the Center. We'll look for loons and comical little tip-ups in the reeds, an' we'll have a look under the butternut tree as we pass by to see if our doors and steps are there all right, an' maybe we'll stop at Shady Rest Cabins, Hamburgers, Antiques for a cone for the Buckles that want cones, or a hamburger for those that feel that way."

Fan was grieved, however, when she got up in the cool of the next morning to discover her mother filling tin tubs and basins at the sink. Two kettles were steaming on the oil stove and Charles was crossing to the sink with more pails that had just been filled at the well in front of the store.

"Fer goodness sake, not baths, Mother," she wailed. "Not on a real Holiday!"

"Don't forget it's Sunday, sweety. The first once scrubbed is the first one over with it. Your basin's ready an' waiting."

"Where?"

Six golden heads blossomed from different corners, waiting to hear the orders of the day. "Fetch the screen from the front room, Charles," said Mrs. Buckle, "and put it around those two basins in the corner, behind the kitchen table. One is for Fan and one is for Delia. Charles, Eddy, George, and little Horace each get a corner of the front room. An' I don't want the soap spared, my muddy turtles. Call out when you're ready for the rinse and I'll come around with a fresh pail and hot kettle."

"I want to scrub in the kitchen, Mother," said little Horace, advancing from the front room, already prepared for the ordeal. "It's hot in there; I want to have my tub right in the doorway."

Mrs. Buckle considered the proposition. "Well, I don't know what harm it'd do," she decided. "Only I was going to start the sandwiches and it'll be kind of crowded out here."

"I won't splash."

"In with you, then."

"I want soap flakes, I don't want that hard old bar soap."

"My land, Horace, you're getting as fussy as the time you had the mumps." Mrs. Buckle chuckled and sprinkled soap flakes into the tin tub beside the doorway. "I hope you won't take it into your head to come down with something before we get settled in our new home. Now then, everybody all set?"

"Okay."

"Then I'll get at the sandwiches."

The tenant house smoked with outcries from every corner, with Fan, as usual, leading all the rest. "Gooseb'ry jam," she clamored, beating on the rim of her tin basin with her own round cake of sweet-smelling pink soap. "Don't forget how I love gooseb'ry jam san'wiches."

"Rozb'ry for me, Mother," said Delia as soon as she could make herself heard.

"Gooseb'ry and rozb'ry coming up. Now, somebody's sure to want cold ham."

"I do." It was Fan again. Her pink soap slid under the screen and she pursued it boldly into the open. "I want loads of ham san'wiches all sopping soakin' with salad dressing."

George appeared in the doorway. "So do I, Mother," he shouted. "I love dressin'."

Mrs. Buckle turned her head for a long cold look. "So do I, deary," she said simply. "On legs as well as on sandwiches. And from now on I don't want any lad in my kitchen without his pants," she warned firmly. Turning, her eyes caught little Horace's surprised stare. "And that goes for you, too, son," she made haste to add. "The very minute you are through with those suds you twist yourself into a towel and scuttle into the other room for Charles

to help you dry and dress. Now, let's see, where was I?"

The alphabet knew. "Ham san'wiches," they reminded her in one voice.

"So I was, ham. Well, that about clears up the sandwich situation. And brings us to spice cookies, and molasses cookies, and dill pickles, and———"

"Bananas," said Eddy. "You forgot them once."

"But I'm never likely to again," chuckled Mrs. Buckle, tucking seven fat bananas into the covered basket. "Anything else?"

"Harr-rr-rrumph!"

A shaggy head appeared in the open doorway and, resting its chin on the sill, cleared its throat loudly. Little Horace was shocked. He stood up in his tub, meeting the head eye to eye, and stuck out his tongue. A hand reached up beside the head and laid a peppermint ball on little Horace's tongue. The youngest Buckle dropped back into his tub with a splash and drew his suds about him.

"Moth-er-r!" he choked and lisped, owing to the size of the peppermint ball. "Moth-er-r, here ith 'at mathithan again. Han'ker'thif an' all."

"Quite correct, my man. Handkerchief and all." The shaggy head waggled around on the sill curiously. "Always keep your eye on the handkerchief. But for all of that, you'll find that the hand is quicker than the eye."

And it was. How, nobody knew, but another hand did shoot into the air and a hail of peppermint drops spattered about the floor of the little tenant house. Nobody cared

about watching the handkerchief after that. Every corner
blossomed with golden heads and a few spidery little pink
legs slithered into view. They did not escape the sharp
eye of Fan, even from behind her screen.

"Moth-er-r," she cried. "No fair for Horace and George
to hunt pep'mint balls until we all can; make 'em get back
into their tubs."

Delia was no less indignant. "You know what you said
about pants, Mother," she cried.

"And that's no magician, Horace Buckle," Fan added
for good measure. "Magicians shake bunnies out of their
hats, not pep'mint balls, or sausages, or whatever out of
their pocket handkerchiefs. That's the man that lives next
door to Mr. Moom and has a stick garden."

"So you think you know me, eh?" The shaggy head
soared above the sill, higher and higher. The man must
have found the orange box with his groping feet and lifted
himself by means of it from the bog to the trailer. "You,
whoever you are, think I'm no magician, eh? Well then,
just you hark to this!

> Fee—fi—fo—foam!
> There'll be bunnies in my home
> The next time you and Horace see
> A rainbow in a white birch tree.
> And if you're brave you'll come arunning
> Down the street to me."

"Law me!" A little more of Fan than she would have

allowed under quieter circumstances oozed forth from behind the screen. "Is that an invitation?" she buzzed.

"It wouldn't be more legal if it was written."

"Well, what do you know." She was almost too exasperated for words. She needed a good spin on her toes but there was no room in the corner, of course, with Delia and two tin tubs of water. "The way things happen to us," she spluttered. "Yesterday nothing to do and nowhere to go. And today, a Holiday and baths—not that they are any treat—and another invitation down Braeside. For Horace, of all things. Maybe if we didn't have to go away so soon, Charles and Delia and Eddy would be invited, too, and the folks would get acquainted with us."

"What do you mean, go away so soon?"

"Why, when Mr. Watson comes home he's going to move us down the road."

"By gorry, that reminds me—road." Mr. Liggard poked his head inside the kitchen and looked around. "Is there a lad named—I mean, is Eddy here?" he asked.

The Buckles were still. Far be it from them to reveal Eddy's corner to any stranger unless they knew more about what was in the wind. Eddy could never be suspected of being in trouble, but Eddy had a collection of Vics that could be suspected of almost anything, and the Buckles protected their own whether they approved of them or not. Even Mrs. Buckle watched this queer visitor sharply and was speechless until she saw him nod at her and wink from behind little Horace's wet back. Then she said:

"Eddy, lovey, you're wanted. Come on out."

"I can't, Mother," was the worried reply.

"You sure can, son. Hustle out and no more words about it, if you please."

Eddy obeyed promptly, then. He was dried, combed, and shirted, but he carried his pants in his hand. "You said you didn't want any lad in your kitchen without these," he explained. "I brought them, but I didn't have time to put 'em on."

Mr. Liggard whooped so suddenly and so thunderously that little Horace rose from his tub and, clad only in a shimmer of clinging suds, fled to the front room and the protection of Charles.

"You're the Buckle who owns a horse, I understand," said Mr. Liggard then, a trifle less boisterously.

"Yes, sir."

"Well, I waded around through this mire to tell you that you won't have one any longer unless you're a first-class runner."

Eddy was too shocked to reply, so Mr. Liggard continued without being urged. "I got up early for a bit of a stroll around," he explained, "and there was that horse ambling along the County Road toward The Center, with his little green cart bumping along behind and a rope trailing in the dust. He must have pulled himself free of whatever he was tied to."

"Why-y, the old meanie." Fan's shrill cry cut across all other sounds. "All hitched up to take us on a Holiday and just when we get all lathered and under the water he goes off alone. After all the buckets of boiled potato parings we fed him yesterday, too."

Eddy said nothing. He skimmed above Mr. Liggard's head like a bat in dogdays and landed in the bog with a plop-p-p.

"Golly," cried George from the front room. "I heard Eddy clear in here. Look out the door, somebody, an' see what happened. He could maybe be way under the mud an' all covered up."

"Only he isn't," Mr. Liggard assured everybody. "He's up and out on the road, traveling like Oliver Binns when he smells fish in the neighborhood."

"Humph!" Fan didn't care for the picture. But a happier thought brought her golden head into view again. "It's a mercy Eddy had his pants in his hand and not on him, wasn't it, Mother?" she said. "Poor Eddy. He'll have to take another bath, now, when he comes home. Hurry up an' dry my back, Delia."

"Ss-sssh!"

"What for? Mr. Liggard has gone."

It was the good word that the Buckle alphabet was waiting for. They squirmed out of their hidden corners and surged up to the kitchen table. "No Holiday, eh?" gloomed George. "After all that scrubbin'."

"Why of course we'll have a Holiday, sweety," chuckled Mrs. Buckle. "Why not?"

"With Mark and Eddy gone?"

"They'll come back."

"But it'll be too late to go to Aunty Belle's."

"That could be."

"Hurray-y-y!" George pulled off the necktie that was hanging loosely about his neck and snapped it across the back of a chair. "Where will we go, Mother?"

"Oh, we'll think of a place. It isn't where we go that makes a Holiday, remember; it's——"

"The baths. I know."

"It's doing something different and having a grand time at it, my lad." Mrs. Buckle clapped shut the lid of the picnic basket and wiped her hands. "If you can say at sundown, 'My, wasn't this a grand day, we won't forget it as long as we live!' why then you've had a worthwhile Holiday. And I don't know what we're wasting time for. Let's get at it. Empty those tin tubs and basins, wipe them out, hang up the towels."

"But, Mother!" Fan couldn't believe her ears. "We can't start without Eddy."

"Who's even thinking of such a thing, sweety? I told you we'd have something different, and we will. We'll begin by sitting in a row on the doorsill of our own kitchen and having a real sharp look at the swale while we try that new bird game I was telling you about the other day, the one we never got around to playing yet. I'll sit at one end and Delia at the other, and George, Fan, and Horace, you squeeze in between. It's a good thing we are all littles."

"Where's Charles going to sit?" asked Fan.

"I guess he'll have to stand, lovey, and look over our shoulders."

"Golly, I can't see anything," howled little Horace, smothering under the press of kinfolks. "Make Charles get back farther, Mother."

"You'll see all right in a minute, son, as soon as we're settled. Now then, Fan, I'll have those peppermint balls, if you please."

Fan would have jumped if she had had room. As it was, she opened the pocket in her pink sunsuit and rolled six balls into her mother's hand with a sigh. "The rest are in my towel," she confessed sheepishly.

"I thought as much. Fetch 'em here, Charles, and shake 'em out in my lap. So-o-o, all ready? Then here we go. The first Buckle to see a bird and name it correctly gets a Prize peppermint ball and the one who gets none has only himself to blame because the swale is full of birds this morning. Go-o-o!"

"Wren," snapped Charles. Fan questioned his brightness at once.

"You do not see a wren," she cried. "Where?"

"Under the leaf where it's wiggling on the silky dogwood."

"I see it. Humming bird, on the sow thistle."

"Goldfinch."

"Hey-y, that makes two for Charles already, Mother."

"Good for Charles."

"Redwing," shouted George.

"Redwing it is, lovey." Mrs. Buckle was dealing out candy balls faster and faster.

"Kingfisher, nuthatch, and loon," cried Delia. "My goodness, look at that loon, he's as big as one of Mr. Watson's turkeys all stuffed for Christmas dinner. I ought to get two peppermints for a loon, Mother."

"One peppermint, one bird," ruled Mrs. Buckle gaily. "Who's next?"

"Flicker."

Fan drew herself up and away from the doorsill. "Law me, the things you see, Charles Buckle," she sputtered. "You sit down there and let me stand—— Oh my goodness, two bluebirds, a gull, and a sparrow."

"Sparrows don't count."

"Don't sparrows count, Mother?"

"I don't know why not. They're birds."

"But—but they aren't Prize birds." Charles felt there was a difference. "Sparrows are all over the place. I bet you I've seen ten already."

"Too bad you didn't name them, deary."

"Julia," roared little Horace.

"And don't let Charles tell you Julia isn't a bird," sniffed Fan, eyeing the puddle under the elderberries suspiciously. "Of course, if it's a hell-diver an' not Julia——"

"But it is Julia." George had no doubts on that subject. "Look at the way she splashes. She's having more fun than when she swims in our new dish pan, do you know it?"

"How did she get out of the scrub bucket under the sink?"

"She just blew out of it when Eddy flew through the kitchen. I saw her kind of come unstuck from Katy and Lulu, but I don't know how she got down over the trailer into the swale."

"Get her, Charles, she'll run off and lose herself." Delia was worried.

"Papa Robin and three babies." Fan's shout startled the alphabet. And then, following the direction of her pointing finger, they frothed with giggles.

"Look at 'em." George doubled over and choked. "See Papa strut. An' the way the babies hop along behind him in a straight line, like soldiers on parade. That's just what it is, a Robin Parade."

"We'll be the music for 'em!" hummed Fan. "Come on.

> Tum, tum, te, tum,
> Strike up the band,
> Here comes the best Robin troop in the land!
> We'll never halt,
> We'll never turn,
> We'll follow Pa till he digs up a worm!"

"Here comes Eddy," shouted little Horace.

And nobody ever did know what happened to the Robin Parade. The Buckles were on their feet instantly, staring at the County Road with popping eyes. "Where's Eddy?" asked Charles.

"Don't you see Mark?" Fan was impatient at Charles' slowness in putting two and two together to make four. "If that's Mark, that's got to be Eddy sitting up there behind his old switching tail, driving him as nice as——"

"There are two somebodys in Nero."

"Oh sure, one is Vaughn."

"That cat's name isn't Vaughn, Fan Buckle."

"What difference does it make. He's as black as two nights before dawn. And he'd just as quick have a fit on our lawn as anywhere else, I bet you."

George lined up with the menfolks. "That other somebody is black, too," he pointed out. "Eddy's head is as yellow as——"

"Oh puff! It wouldn't be yellow if it had a black thing on it, would it? If Eddy was wearing Mr. Hooke's scarecrow's hat, the one he blesses the leeks and onions with—ooo-hooo, Eddy. We don't have to go to The Center. It's too late."

Eddy guided Mark from the road to the swale and shouted as the ridgy horse gave no indication of stopping beside the trailer. "Catch hold of his rope, Charles, an' loop it around the hook as we come by," he begged. The sudden halt unseated him, but Nero's back proved its worth and it was not necessary for the family to pick Eddy out of the ditch this time.

"We don't have to go to The Center," Fan announced for the second time.

Eddy looked at her with lackluster eyes. "I've been to The Center," he said soberly.

"But what made you take the scarecrow's hat away from him? Mr. Hooke's going to be awful mad. First the crows peck it, an' then Vaughn pulls it to pieces, an' now Eddy just naturally takes it away."

"I didn't take it away from any scarecrow. I took it away from Oliver, he was stuck in it."

"Stuck in——"

"Hush, Fan." Mrs. Buckle leaned out of the doorway and urged Eddy to climb the orange box and have a pitcher of cold lemonade. "You're hot, lovey," she said. "And tired to death. Don't tell me you had to chase Mark all the way to The Center."

"As far as Shady Rest Cabins, Hamburgers, Antiques."

"Was that horse hungry again?" George couldn't believe it.

"I don't know, I didn't wait to see. Mr. Wente came out and stopped him for me and turned him around and gave him a slap, just to start him off after I climbed inside Nero and pulled my pants on. We'd have come home flying then, only for a man who popped up out of the ditch and fired a rock at us."

"A rock at you, lovey?"

"Yes'm. It hit Nero right on his nightgown. But the man didn't mean any harm; he was chasing a cat, he said, and came out of the house so fast he forgot to put on his spectacles. He just let fly at the first thing he saw moving in front of him and he was kind of surprised, I can tell you, when the thing kept coming toward him instead of running the other way and he saw it was Mark and Nero and me."

"I can well believe it, deary."

"He reached in his pocket and found his spectacles then, and put them on, and said, 'My word, a Buckle!' And then he said, 'Which one?' And I told him I was Eddy. And he said, 'Gad! I'd give fifty cents to know how that horse blew Moom down, the other afternoon!' "

"Fifty cents," shrilled Fan. "Law me, Eddy's Vics are beginning to earn money for the Chests already. Did you tell him, Eddy?"

"I said fifty cents was a fair price, but it was a secret. And he promised he'd keep it faithfully. So then I yelled MAG-you-know-what at the top of my voice and my gosh, what do you think happened?"

"Mark sneezed."

Eddy looked at Fan coldly. "That's a smart guess," he said. "Of course Mark sneezed. He sneezed this hat right out from under a hedge, and Oliver Binns was stuck inside it. So the man said, 'There's that danged cat, and that's my hat!' He held Oliver's tail and I yanked at the brim and we got 'em apart after a while. Only both of 'em were kind of ruined. This man, his name is Mr. Hooke and he lives down Braeside next to Oliver and he isn't so bad when you know him, Mother."

"Most folks aren't, sweety. What were you going to say about Mr. Hooke?"

"He said he'd add another ten cents to the fifty for my war work if I'd take the cat and the hat out of his sight, and that's what I'm doing."

"What's his scarecrow going to do without a hat?" Fan demanded.

"I thought about that, too. Mother, do your remember that little bonnet with the green lilacs and the purple veil that Aunty Belle gave you for Easter?"

"I wish I could forget it, lovey."

"I told Mr. Hooke about it and I told him if you didn't want it any more he could have it for his scarecrow. And he said if a little bonnet with green lilacs and a purple veil wouldn't teach Oliver Binns and the One-Tree Island crows to keep their distance, nothing would. So then he invited me to come down Braeside."

"Invited you, Eddy?" Fan repeated the word, awed.

"He said he would take it as a great kindness if I'd drop in and knot the bonnet streamers and adjust the veil as soon as possible."

"Did you tell him we wouldn't be here after today, Eddy?"

"No." Eddy reached for the pitcher of lemonade. "No, I didn't," he said slowly. "Because I am going to be here. Even if Mr. Watson pulls our house down the road, I'm coming back to Braeside every day. Because Mark and Nero and I have a job here."

7. A Slanting Pasture

Mrs. Buckle brushed Charles off the kitchen stool and sat down upon it, herself. "You—you have a job, deary?" she asked. "Here in Braeside?"

"Yes'm. Mark an' Nero an' me."

"What kind of a job, Eddy? You're a good worker, but you are not very big, you know."

"Mark an' Nero an' me, we can do collectin' all right."

"Collecting? Collecting what?"

"I don't believe you ever took a good look at that street, Mother."

"I did," Fan interrupted suddenly. "And so did George. Messy, that's what it is. Trash piles everywhere."

"Mr. Hooke said if I'd keep him raked up out in front," Eddy continued soberly, "and haul his hedge clippings away down the road somewhere, and I can do it now, you know, since I nailed that back onto Nero, he'd pay me fifty cents each week."

"Fifty cents, not every week, Eddy?" It was Fan, of course. "Not four times fifty, not two dollars every month for the Chests, Eddy Buckle?"

"It'll be more than that. Mr. Hooke said he'd call on

the neighbors and put it up to them straight that it was time Braeside had a hand in this war work and the Chests of Cheer would be a fine place to begin, especially since they'd get a clean street in the bargain. I told him that I'd speak to Mr. Watson about cleaning up in front of his vacant lot."

"Eight lots to keep clean. Eight times two is———"

"I'm not counting on eight." Eddy had another drink of lemonade. "Mr. Moon isn't expected to be interested."

"Why not, fer goodness' sake? Oh, I know, MAGGIE." Fan giggled wildly. "Well, let him keep his old trash piles outside his gate if he wants to. Seven times two is—is fourteen dollars every month. Boy-y-y, Eddy'll have the war all taken care of before our Vics even begin to work."

"Julia's beginning," Delia reminded her gently.

"One egg, sometimes." Fan waved the thought of Julia away with a flirt of her fingers. "Eddy, can I help you collect? I could hang onto Nero's back and yell, 'Trash, tra-a-a-ash! Bring out your nice prickly clippings, your dried hollyhock stalks an' cabbage stumps, tra-a-a-ash!'"

"Fan! My goodness, lovey."

"They'd hear me, wouldn't they?"

"They'd hear you across the border. But, Eddy, when school begins———"

"I know. I thought of that too. That's why Mr. Watson mustn't haul our house too far away. I'll find time after school, with somebody to help. Maybe Charles could be my partner."

"Don't forget I've got Imogene to look after," Charles reminded him. "What you going to do when the gardens are all cleaned up and snow comes, Eddy?"

"Mr. Hooke said he'd always wanted to make a little snowplow out in his shop but he'd never got around to it yet; he said it would be lots more fun with a nice little boy to help him and learn how to use tools; he said we'd make lots of things and——"

"Who did he mean, 'we'?"

"Me, of course. I might be down in Braeside most of the time from now on, Mother. And oh, that makes me think, Mr. Hooke said that he didn't believe we'd see Mr. Watson around here tomorrow."

"Why not, deary?"

"On account of what happened out in the ocean. He cut the picture out of the Sunday paper for me. See that big boat standing on its nose?" Eddy spread a sheet of crumpled paper on the kitchen table while the alphabet crowded close. "That's the ship that was bringing the little children from over where the war is."

"What happened to it?" cried Fan. "What's it shaking the poor little children off into the water for?"

"It got bombed, that's what."

The Buckles were silent, until Mrs. Buckle whispered, "Dear heaven!"

Eddy laid his hand upon her knee. "Mr. Hooke said for us not to fret too much," he said. "He read out of the paper to me that most all the children and mamas were safe in little boats and on rafts and things like that; they aren't very far away from shore and everybody is on the watch for them when they drift in to land. The only trouble is that they are going to be awfully separated and it'll take some time for the right children to find their mamas, for them all to get together again, don't you see? Mr. Hooke said that if some of Mr. Watson's family drifted ashore and were brought to Gananoque, but some were still floating out on the ocean, why, he'd likely wait right there until—until——"

"Until those who have been frightened and parted are brought together in safety and comforted," said Mrs. Buckle quietly. "Of course he'll wait and help where he can."

"And we'll pray to God tonight to keep His Eye on the rafts and things," added Fan briskly. "I guess with God and Mr. Watson watching out, they won't be lost long. Oh my goodness, help-p!"

Mr. Binns was arriving, with no more advance notice than a shadow. He lit on the doorsill of the little tenant house, his back peaked, his tail swollen to four times its normal size, all claws bared, siss-ss-ss-ssing his meanest. Happening to find himself nearest little Horace and remembering the butternut tree, he gathered up a handful of claws and gave this Buckle all he had.

"Eddy!" shrieked Fan.

The war was over, however, before Eddy could move. Horace simply stiffened his leg, stuck one tiny slipper into Mr. Binns's thick fur, and pushed. And Oliver slid into the swale.

"Scat-t-t!" said little Horace for good measure. "Of all the sassy—hey-y, Mother, when are we going to have our Holiday? I'm hungry."

"We're on our way this very minute, lovey," chuckled Mrs. Buckle, springing to her feet and reaching for the covered basket. "Put a couple of blankets, some cushions, and this in Nero, Eddy, and let's see how nice Mark can climb the slanting pasture out back. I think it'll feel pretty nice to sit high for a change, high and dry. Away up to the very top of the pasture with our backs to the pine woods and the sun in our faces. After we eat all the sandwiches, maybe we can fill the basket with pine cones and take them with us to our new home where, I hope, we'll have something cheerier than oil to cook by. Cones make the dandiest, snappiest fire you ever heard on a cold morning."

"Do we have to take the Vics?" asked George, hoping for the best.

"I don't know why not, deary. They'll enjoy a change as much as the rest of us. Lift the bucket with Julia, Katy, and Lulu into Nero and——"

"Help-p-p!" Watching Eddy drop from the trailer to the orange box, Fan glimpsed more than she bargained for and lifted her voice again in shrill warning. "That awful Vaughn's climbing into Nero too, Eddy," she cried. "He can't have a Holiday with us."

"Mother just said that our Vics could go." Eddy reached up for the covered basket and swung that from the trailer to the box. "Only maybe Julia, Katy, an' Lulu wouldn't enjoy themselves so much, unless you could tie a quilt over the bucket. Why don't you just leave them at home, under the sink?"

"But they are Vics, Eddy Buckle. They belong to our alphabet. That cat doesn't."

"He might."

"Be a Vic? Belong to us? Earn money for the Chests?"

"Maybe. Of course he won't really belong to us, but we might pretend just while he's being a Vic. We're down to N-is-Nero, and the next letter is O, isn't it? O-is-Oliver."

"Fer gosh sakes!" George turned to his twin, his eyes blazing. "That's what comes of wishing on a lily, Fan Buckle," he pointed out.

"Don't tell me that I wished anything about that spittin' old Vaughn, George, 'cause I never did."

"You wished that we'd earn more money for the Chests, didn't you? An' look what happened to Eddy right away. An' you wished we'd have more alphabet, an' there's your cat."

"She'd better not wish anything about me," Charles warned sternly. "Was that all, George?"

"No. She wished we'd live in Braeside forever and ever."

"Oh well, that's nothing to worry about, not with Mr. Moom there. She could have left that off about the alphabet, though."

"Law me!" Fan's voice rose to a high pitch. "What letter comes after O, Eddy?" she demanded.

"P."

"Do we know any P's?"

"No."

"Well, thank goodness. I'll never make any more magic wishes." Fan went the limit in trying to undo the damage she had wrought in Lily Bay. "Except, maybe, if I had a lily now I'd say I don't care whether we earn any more money for the Chests or not, and I certainly don't want to be squeezed up forever and ever in a fussy, messy little street like Braeside, and I don't, I don't, I don't want any more alphabet!"

Notwithstanding its forlorn beginning the Holiday turned out to be fun, after all. It was different. And it was a day the Buckles were sure they would never forget.

They climbed the slanting pasture to the very top and there they tied Imogene and Mark to pine trees, spread their blankets over buttercups, daisies, harebells, and purple vetch, and opened the covered basket. Then, with a sandwich in each hand, they leaned back into the hollows made by upheaved pine roots and looked about. It was a surprise to all of them.

"Why, it's like being in the balcony at a movie," said Delia, forgetting to eat. "We can look right down into all the Braeside gardens; inside the hedges, I mean. And straight through the street to the dock. And all the river beyond, the islands and the fishing boats."

"That's THE MOLLY down by the dock," whooped George. "It doesn't look any bigger than a butter dish from here."

"And the little tenant house is like a cereal box," giggled Fan. "And the County Road is the long white string that tied it up before it came loose."

"What's that white line from the gate to the front door in the second yard down there?" asked Delia.

"Roses." Fan wiped a drop of salad dressing from her wrist. "A whole border of white baby roses. That's where Mrs. Mold lives. She's not a very cheerful woman, Captain Todd thinks. Horace's magician lives in the next house. Boy-y-y, I hope it rains before we have to move away from the swale."

"Why do you?"

"You heard Mr. Liggard say that if Horace and I found a rainbow in the birch tree we could come and see him, didn't you? I want to hear about his sticks."

"What sticks?"

"His story sticks. The garden's full of 'em. They hold up his geraniums and petunias and things, but they've all got stories to them, like maybe the one that came from the house that Jack built."

"Not really, Fan?"

"I've got a story stick!" little Horace announced suddenly. "It's about a

> Sassy little duck
> Who said, 'quack, quack,
> No other duck's got a
> Curl on his back!'

Tell me the rest of the story, Fan."

Fan was indignant. "I should say not," she said. "I came on a Holiday to eat san'wiches, not to tell that old story over and over again. And besides, you haven't got a real story stick; that thing of yours was only a handle to Mrs. Watson's umbrella, once."

"It's got an Impy duck on it. And a story about——"

"Oh, go on, Fan, tell him," said Mrs. Buckle comfortably. "It won't hurt any of us to remember that impolite little duck now and then."

"It won't hurt Horace, anyway," said George.

Horace was grieved. This wasn't the way his story hours usually began. "I'm not impolite," he howled.

"You stuck your tongue out at Mr. Liggard this morning. What do you call that?"

Horace recalled the incident with almost too much sorrow and shame. He cast his dill pickle into George's lap and himself into Mrs. Buckle's. "I didn't mean to be sassy," he choked. "I didn't mean to be."

His mother patted the back of his golden head comfortingly. "Of course you didn't, lovey," she said. "Of course you didn't. And you're going to tell Mr. Liggard so the first chance you get. The best of us are apt to make mistakes at times, especially if we get surprised in our suds. How about that Impy duck, Fan?"

Fan swallowed the last of her ham sandwich and wiped her fingers on a clump of harebells. "Well-l, just this once," she gave fair warning. "After this, Horace has got to remember his own stories, or have George tell him.

Now, this little black duck, sir, alas and alack,
Was the most impolite thing that ever said 'quack!'
He roamed down the garden paths, he roamed through the
    roses,
He tripped fat old gentlemen upon their fat old noses.

"That's just what he did one morning to Farmer Brown while Farmer Brown was all snarled up in his bathrobe, 'cause he'd been out in the kitchen———"

"Frying sausages!" interrupted little Horace, surging up from his mother's lap entirely recovered from his late attack of doldrums. "He had a long-handled fork in his hand and he'd been frying sausages."

Fan stared. This was a new slant on an old story. "Who said so?" she demanded.

"My magician did. He said he'd been out in his kitchen frying——"

"Oh, all right. Anyway, Farmer Brown had been out in his kitchen doing something, when along comes a little black duck, skips right between his feet, and trips him up as neat as you please. Down he plopped, bingo!

"Of course he got right up again, and what he had to say to that little black duck was plenty.

But all the little duck did was to laugh and to shout,
'If you haven't got a curl on your back you're out!'

"And of course Farmer Brown didn't. He didn't have a curl anywhere, being perf'c'ly bald on top. What was on his back nobody could see, of course, on account of the bathrobe only it wasn't any curl, I bet you.

"Well-l, the little black duck hustled off scratching cinders, sod, and gravel this way and that like sixty never mind who's eye got in the way. He was always scratching around the barnyard like that. It got so anybody could look down and say, 'Oh ho, so that impolite Duck's been around again. Scratched his name all over everything.'

"Now, on this very morning that Farmer Brown was—was——"

"Frying sausages in his kitchen," little Horace insisted firmly.

Fan caught her breath, but wasted none of it in

argument. "All right," she continued. "On this very morning that Farmer Brown was doing something in his kitchen
and was upset on his fat old nose, Impy scampered away,
tickled pink over what he had done, and headed straight
for the cornstalk where Grandfather Grasshopper lived.
He had wanted for the longest time to kick a cinder into
Grandfather Grasshopper's eye and that shows what kind
of a duck Impy was, 'cause if he had been smart he would
have known that was something that couldn't be done.
Grandfather G. was up on the roof of his cornstalk an'
perf'c'ly safe before Impy was anywhere near his cellar
door in the root. Of course he was mad. He leaned over
an' bawled Impy out something awful, but the little black
duck just laughed.

'If you want to boss things 'round this farm,' he said,
    'quack!
You've got to wear feathers that curl on your back!'

And you know how many feathers a Grasshopper wears.

"So then he came to the stump where Cock-of-the-Walk
was roosting, and Cock-of-the-Walk has just as many
feathers, I bet you, as little black ducks do. Only they
don't curl up on his back. They droop down as nice an'
smooth as you please, 'cause Cock-of-the-Walk is very,
very polite. That's what fooled Impy. He thought nobody
could be polite and boss things, too. So he up an' scratched
a hunk of gravel right smack against Cock-of-the-Walk's
beak and did it sting! An' Cock got right down from that
stump.

'So it's the feather that curls on your back that's to blame?
Dear me—doodle-ooo!' said he. 'My, what a shame!
I wonder why we keep such rude kids about
When it's perf'c'ly easy to pull those curls out!'

"An' boy-y-y, he did it! One yank was enough. Out came the feather an' Cock-of-the-Walk shook it off his beak onto the path where the little black duck had been scratchin' his name everywhere, Impolite, Impolite, Impolite. And what do you think happened?"

"I know," little Horace confessed honestly, "but I'm not going to tell you."

"You don't have to, I'm telling the story now." Fan accepted a spice cooky, folded her hands over it for future reference, and continued. "When that feather, that curly feather, shook off of Cock's beak it fell right between the I and the M on the path and there it stuck. And what it did to Impy's name was puh-lenty. It changed it, that's all. The whole farmyard saw that now, instead of being Impolite, the word had become I'm polite!

"Impy was shocked. All the oompah went right out of him with a big siss-ss-s. 'My goodness,' he quacked, 'I don't want to be the I'm polite duck. Where's the fun?'

"He found out that there was fun in being polite, though. People liked him and said right to his face that he was a credit to the family and the little black duck thought that was a lot of fun, after he was accustomed to it. But the thing that made him really proud enough to bust was what Grandfather Grasshopper said. 'Don't it beat the dickens,' he said, 'the difference it makes where a feather is. On that little duck's back, that was all you could see, just a feather. But now, you can see the duck that was under it, and he's growing to look more like Cock-of-the-Walk every day. Gentlemanlike, that's what he is.'

"And after that, Impy kept a sharp eye on his own back; every morning, first thing, he looked it all over up one side and down the other to be sure no feather was beginning to curl up on him. And that's all there is to it, Horace, unless you want to let Charles have a look to see what's going on under the back of your overall suit."

Horace reached for another pickle, thought better of it, and grinned while the rest of the alphabet giggled wildly. Fan laid the spice cooky aside. "I'm not ready for it yet," she explained. "I'm hungry all over again. I think I'll have another ham sandwich, Mother."

"Why, they're all gone, lovey."

"Gone? Who took 'em?"

"It looked as if everybody was finished with sandwiches, so I gave what was left to Eddy for his cat."

"To Eddy? For that mean old—" Fan peeped around a pine tree and saw them, snuggled against each other side by side, the boy's arm around a fat, furry middle and the black head and the gold ear to ear. "Why-y-y, Eddy Buckle," she gasped.

Eddy was undisturbed. "Oliver's nice, when you get acquainted," he said. "He's the biggest cat that ever lived,

I bet you. Come here and listen to him rumble and purr-rr-rrrr way down inside of him; he sounds like the motor in Mr. Watson's car."

"He could have the whole car in him and I wouldn't care." Fan drew back with a sniff of disgust. "What makes me mad is the ham san'wiches he's got in him. Boy-y-y, something's the matter with Mark."

Eddy was on his feet instantly, but no quicker than every other member of the Buckle alphabet. Mark, it seemed, had suddenly as many legs as a spider and they were flying in all directions. George whisked behind a pine tree with barely a shimmer of daylight between himself and a lively hoof, and little Horace dropped behind the lemonade pail just before it was hit and sent spinning along down the slanting pasture.

"Golly, has that horse got his strength back," yelled Charles, simply rolling over and over and trusting to luck that he was moving in the right direction. "Eddy, make Mark whoa-a."

Eddy was pained. "You know Mark hasn't learned how to whoa-a yet," he said. "Come and help me bear down on his rope. Well, no wonder the poor old feller kicked; I should say something was the matter with him. Look here, will you, he's got a biting cockchafer in his nose and a prickly cocklebur on his ear."

"Not both at once." Fan was inclined to think the report exaggerated. "Why would he?"

"Why would—you don't think Mark hurt his nose and

ear on purpose, do you? Hold still, poor old feller; there,
I got the cocklebur off, but I can't get the cockchafer out
of his nose. There, there, Mark, we'll help you, don't
you worry any more."

Fan moved out from behind the sheltering covered basket and took a deep breath. "MAGG-GG-GGIE!" she directed
at the top of her lungs.

And suddenly so much happened that nobody could
tell what came first or later. Mark sneezed, and Eddy blew
away across the harebells like a lopped-off dandelion blossom. Mark sneezed again, and George and Delia and
Horace were scattered to the winds. Mark sneezed a
third time and Mrs. Buckle said, "Another one like that
and he'll shake himself apart. He'll go up in dust!"

But there wasn't any other one like that. Mark was
through. He leaned up against his pine tree and fell asleep
at once.

"There," said Fan smugly. "Got rid of his old cockchafer as nice as you please."

"Fan Buckle, if you ever—if you ever——"

"But, Eddy, you didn't want Mark to live forever and
ever with a biting old cockchafer in his nose, did you?"
she asked.

"Of course not. But if you ever——"

"Phooey, I won't, don't fret. I just wanted to show him
how he could do himself some good with that old sneeze,
maybe. If Mark's going around this pasture putting

cockchafers in his nose, he ought to know how to get 'e.
out again."

"Likely he'll never be here again."

"He might. If we lived here, he would."

"If we lived—— Don't be silly." The Buckles picked
themselves up and returned to their cushions. "Mr. Watson couldn't pull the little tenant house up this slanting
pasture, over the rocks and all," Charles pointed out.

"Who wants his old tenant house." Fan didn't, certainly, the alphabet found out almost at once. "He could
build us a long white house right here, with its back
against the pine trees and a porch all the way along its
front. We could have sheds out back all over the place for
the Vics. And whenever Mother wanted to watch the river
and the little green islands and the white sailboats, she
wouldn't have to peek under the shade at our kitchen window. She could come right out on the porch and sit wherever she wanted to. And we could sit here on the steps
with her and look down into Braeside and watch the folks
in their gardens, and THE MOLLY at the dock, and——
boy-y-y, I like a slanting pasture, do you know it?"

8. Charles and Delia Are Welcomed to Braeside

"MARK's got to be shown how to whoa-a," said George the next morning.

The alphabet agreed. "You bet he has." Charles remembered the day before with a shudder. "How to whoa-a and how to gaddup."

"That old horse knows how to gaddup already," Delia said, nervously. "I wouldn't teach him any more about that, Eddy."

Fan walked away from the group under the elderberries and looked Mark over. "He doesn't know so much about it without a cockchafer in his nose, Delia," she decided. "Go on and tell him to gaddup, Eddy, and see if he even opens his eyes."

"I'd better tell him to whoa-a first; it'd be safer." Eddy's faith in Mark's smartness was slow to die. "Whoa-a, Mark!" he shouted. Mark sighed gently and rubbed his neck along a silky dogwood branch. "There, see?" said Eddy proudly. "He whoa-ed all right."

"He *was* whoa-ed. Tell him to gaddup."

"Aw, Fan, not right after he's had his breakfast, have a heart."

"Then I will. Gaddup, Mark!"

Mark snored.

"He's got to be taught," said Charles firmly. "Boost little Horace up on the trailer, Delia, so he won't get hurt. And toss me down that piece of rope on the hook outside the kitchen door."

He fastened the long rope by its middle to Mark's collar, leaving a knotted end hanging on either side of the ridgy back. "You get into Nero, Eddy," he explained, "and do the driving and the calling out; Mark probably would rather have you boss him. Delia and I will grab hold of the knots on this side, and, Fan and George, you take the rope on the other side. Now then, Delia and Fan and George, stand away from Mark as far as the rope will let you, and run along the side of the road while Eddy's driving; when he says, 'Whoa-a!' everybody swing down on the ropes hard. That'll make Mark stop to think. When Eddy says, "Gaddup!' ease up on the ropes and run along the road like sixty. Mark'll catch on after a while."

"Suppose he gaddups when Eddy says 'Whoa-a,' " Delia asked nervously. "Mark could get mixed up just at first, I should think."

"Then we'll all drop off his ropes into the ditch. He won't run very far."

"No farther than Shady Rest Cabins, Hamburgers, Antiques!" said Fan pointedly.

Captain Todd came out of the corner house to stand on the store steps and watch what was going on. "Well, sir, this beats anything I ever saw in all my life, dod blast me if it don't," he announced. "What's the idea, mates? I thought you treated your Vics like kinfolks."

"We do," George panted, dropping off his rope for a breathing spell. "We aren't hurting Mark. All the Buckles have to go to school, you know, and we're only teaching M-is-Mark how to be a good horse."

"He's learning the hard way, if you ask me."

"Well, but if he's going to be a Vic and haul trash— you know about Eddy's new job, don't you?"

"I do, but does Mark? I bet you he does."

"You mean, hey-y-y, you don't mean that Marks knows how to gaddup. That he'd gaddup and whoa-a if he wanted to?"

"I'm not accusing anybody, I'm just looking on. And by gorry, did you see that?"

George did. He saw Mark, with nobody bearing down on his side ropes, stop so suddenly that Eddy was bounced high into the air. "He d'lib'r'tly did that," howled George.

"He d'lib'r'tly did," echoed Fan. "Mark jounced Eddy pretty near to the moon. There, Charles gave him a good spank for it; served him right, too."

Mark turned his head, saw what had landed on his rear wasn't a horsefly but an angry little fist, snorted gently, and winked at Charles. George and Fan stared at the captain. "Did he, did Mark d'lib'r'tly——" they stammered.

Captain Todd wiped a grin away with the back of his hand. "I'm ready to swear that that horse of yours doesn't do anything without he has his reason for it," he said solemnly. "That's a smart one, no mistake about it. He's having his bit of fun today, likes to have a fuss made over him and excitement all around. He knows how to stop and go all right, all right, when he wants to. How about another fishing trip with me to Lily Bay tomorrow, mates?"

Fan shook her head. "I don't believe we can, sir," she said. "Eddy's going to begin his job of collecting, maybe. And George and me, well, we couldn't get down to the dock without being seen if all the trash heaps were carted away. Of course, if it rains———"

"What's a storm got to do with it?"

"Mr. Liggard said if Horace and I found a rainbow in the birch tree at the bend in the road, we could come down to his house."

"Well-l-l, the old walrus!"

"Of course if we got that far we could maybe crawl to the dock because Mr. Moom's heaps will be right on his walk, same as ever."

"What makes you think that?"

"He doesn't want us down Braeside, sir. He doesn't like Mark, and he doesn't like children, and oh, he doesn't like lots of things. I hope it rains tomorrow before Mr. Watson comes to move us away because little Horace wants to see Mr. Liggard's story sticks and give him a present. And maybe somebody would invite Delia and Charles down the street, then we all would know what Braeside was like. Delia wants to see Mrs. Mold's baby roses. It's funny if nobody would like Delia and Charles. You like George an' me, an' Mr. Hooke likes Eddy, an' Mr. Liggard likes Horace even if he did stick his tongue out at him."

"Mr. Liggard stuck his tongue out at Horace?"

"No, oh my goodness, no! It was Horace's tongue an' he wishes he'd kept it where it belongs, I bet you. Mother told him that no wonder the Braeside folks didn't like the Buckles if they thought all children were as impolite as that. Only we aren't, you know; it's just 'cause Horace was s'prised in his suds. He's going to tell Mr. Liggard how ashamed he is. I hope it rains tomorrow."

"It will," Captain Todd assured her. "I've got a corn that warns me of hail, gales, high water, and visiting relatives. The signals are all for wet weather in the morning."

Nobody will ever forget how it rained that night. It seemed as if the river stood on its side to spill itself upon the County Road. Thunder rolled until the ground trembled and the lids of the stove in the little tenant house lifted and banged. And if the Buckles hadn't been well anchored among the elderberries in the swale they would have been blown away nobody knows where, trailer and all. It was lucky for them that night, they found out, that Mr. Watson had left the little tenant house edged around with its opened door to the swale, away from the storm that blew up Braeside from the river to the pine woods on the upper pasture. The hail, gale, and rain beat against the kitchen window, but of course that was shut and the shade drawn low. The Buckles, huddled against each other inside, didn't sleep much but they were snug and dry. And the morning brought the loveliest, brightest dawn of the whole summer. The alphabet was up and out early to meet it.

Mrs. Buckle was alone in the kitchen after breakfast, sudsing porridge bowls in the sink, when Eddy climbed up to the doorsill and sat down, Oliver Binns at his side.

"Where's everybody?" asked Eddy.

"Outside, looking over the storm damage, and finding only good." Mrs. Buckle reached for the steaming kettle.

"What good did they find?" Eddy ran over in his mind what he had seen and was ready to argue the subject. "You ought to look at the mess of tree branches down all over Braeside."

"Well, that's good for your job, isn't it? And Charles and Delia happened on a dandy patch of watercress while they were out finding what was left of the swale. They cleaned it and made a dozen nice little bunches to put on the Chest basket over at the store."

"Are they over there now?"

"Probably. Fan was helping them pick the cress out in the swale, but she happened on a rosy Long-purple in full bloom and nothing would do but she had to take it across the road to her old captain."

"Where's George? And little Horace?"

"Down the road."

"What for?"

"Oh, to look for a rainbow in the birch tree. Such kids! Heavens, lovey, is it that cat that smells so?" Mrs. Buckle fanned herself with a corner of her apron. "If it is, push him over where he'll be in a stronger draft. What's he been into?"

"Sardines. I bought him three cans and they're kind of leaking through his skin."

"What you wasting sardines on a cat for, deary?"

"They make him shiny."

"And fat, and smelly." Mrs. Buckle leaned against the sink and considered Mr. Binns. "What do you care how he looks, Eddy?" she asked.

Eddy replied by asking another question. "Today is Tuesday, isn't it, Mother?"

"Sure is, lovey."

"And you'd call Oliver Binns a choice pet, wouldn't you?"

"I'd call him lots of things, Eddy, but I never would have thought of that. Who said it?"

"I don't know, yet. I might not be home at dinnertime today, Mother."

"Going to begin your collecting work, deary?"

"Well-l, kind of. Could I take the covered basket?"

"Our picnic basket? You aren't going to carry trash in a basket, are you, Eddy?"

"No, ma'am. Just Oliver."

Mrs. Buckle gasped and looked down at the sober little face in the doorway searchingly. The E-member of her alphabet was a lad to be trusted, she knew that very well. Queer plans often formed in that wise little head, but they were honest plans if they did not always turn out so well. Eddy preferred not discussing his plans before trying them out; she knew that, too. So she handed down the covered basket from its hook, helped slip the unsuspecting Oliver inside, and slid down to the trailer with it, herself, to hoist it over into Nero while Eddy held Mark as close to the orange box as was possible. After that, Eddy picked up the reins and said, "Gaddup!" firmly. And Mrs. Buckle saw no more of E-is-Eddy, M-is-Mark, N-is-Nero, and O-is-Oliver for a long, long time.

After Mark was safely past Shady Rest Cabins, Hamburgers, Antiques, Eddy extracted a bit of torn paper from his blouse and studied it carefully. The paper had once been a handbill. Later, it had been a written invitation, and then it had served to wrap up odds and ends of oily sardines. There was writing on one side, and printing on the other. Eddy exposed the writing before he thought.

"Pinhooks!" he said, turning the paper over. "That's not it. Here we are. First prize, five dollars, five dollars for a choice pet. It's a good thing I noticed what was printed on the other side of Fan's written invitation and a darned sight better thing that I saved it. Now then, Oliver Binns, you've got your big chance to be a Vic, a Vic in a big way. You'd better come across or there'll be no more fish dinners for you at our house and you'll be dropped right out of our alphabet ker-plump. Five dollars for the Chests of Cheer—gosh!"

Back in the little tenant house Mrs. Buckle took up the steaming kettle and returned to her porridge bowls. "He went down the road," she puzzled, "in the direction of The Center. Now I wonder what's got into Eddy Buckle to cart that old cat off to The Center in such a hurry."

"Mother, look!"

Mrs. Buckle smacked the kettle back on the stove and turned to the opened doorway. Fan's golden head was looming up above the sill and Fan's sliver of a finger was calling attention to her own small neck. A splendid thing hung there, something that looked like a loop of tiny pink rosebuds strung on a golden thread, with a clasp of gold at the back.

"The best things I like in all the world are pink things," she said, awed. "A whole chain of pinky——"

"Fan Buckle! Where did you get that coral necklace?"

"Captain Todd gave it to me."

"Gave it to—oh, Fan! You didn't——"

"Hint? Of course I didn't." Fan waved the idea away blithely. "I just told him how I loved pinky things, an' then I gave him the Long-purple from our swale an' was he tickled. He said nobody had ever given him anything since the time Mr. Mold gave him some poison ivy in a rake he borrowed, but that was a mistake. And then I told him how the Long-purples traveled in somebody's luggage, likely, from England to Australia, and he has traveled from Australia to Braeside, too. Only the Long-purples didn't come with him. They came in some old sheep's wool an' were carried to a woolen mill somewhere that was built on the bank of a stream, an' got tossed out into the wet an' liked it fine. An' so they began to grow all up and down and around wherever there was water enough, an' goodness knows we've got enough in our swale today after the storm last night. Captain Todd likes to have me tell him stories; he said his little girl used to."

"His little girl?"

"Sure. He had one, same as all nice people."

"Where is she, lovey?"

"She went away."

"To—to heaven, sweetheart?"

"Law me, no. She married Mrs. Witchit's little boy and went to Detroit. She's got five little boys now, and Captain Todd says she's always threatening to come back to Braeside for the summer 'cause she's afraid he's lonesome. But he says he's not that lonesome. Only when I was telling him about Australia, and pinky things, why then he remembered that his little girl used to like pinky things and when he was in Australia he bought her this very chain of little pinky roses. Only when she went to Detroit she said it was baby stuff an' left it behind. But I'll never leave it behind, never, never, never! Captain Todd said I was to keep it forever to remember him by, an' he was going to keep the Long-purple to remember me by, an' he told me to always love pinky things. l don't think he meant just coral roses, do you, Mother? Boy-y-y, here comes Charles, running."

"Running? Is Delia with him?"

"No. I forgot to tell you. She said she was going down Braeside to——"

"Delia? Down Braeside?"

"Well, while she was in the store with the bunches of cress, Mrs. Mold came in to see if Mr. Hanley had anything to help a burn on her arm. An' you know how Delia is, right away she told Mrs. Mold what to do to stop the pain and Mrs. Mold asked her if she wouldn't go on home with her and help tie it up with a rag or something, an' of course Delia would. Law me, I forgot to remind her to look at those white baby roses while she was there. Here's Charles."

Charles vaulted into the little kitchen with no more than a pat on the doorsill. "Moth-er-r!" he shouted. "Could I have your hairpin?"

"My hairpin? Why, I haven't seen one of those things in ten years, lovey."

"Yes, you have, the one that's hanging over the oil stove."

"Oh, that one. Well, no, lovey, I don't believe I can spare that hairpin. I'd be sunk if anything should happen to it and the feed pipe on the stove plug at the same time. The only way to open that pipe is to prod it with——"

"That's just what I told Mrs. Witchit."

"Witchit?"

"She's the old gopher that lives next to the store across the street from Captain Todd, Mother. I was just telling you about her."

"She isn't a gopher."

"Well-l, look at her teeth. And didn't she yell for Mr. Watson not to move our house down Braeside? Captain Todd doesn't think she's so hot, either."

"Why, Fan Buckle, I never was more surprised, deary. What does Mrs. Witchit want our hairpin for, Charles?"

"She's got cornbread in the oven, a fish to fry, scalloped potatoes ready to bake, and a berry pie in the tin, and a cousin coming on the noon boat. An' her stove has plugged up on her."

"Well, my goodness, deary, take the hairpin, only be careful of it."

"I will. She said if I fixed her stove she'd consider the job worth a dollar, but I said I didn't want any dollar just——"

"Charles Buckle. Throwing a whole dollar right out of the Chests of Cheer." Fan was highly indignant, and surprised to find there was good even in a Mrs. Witchit.

"Maybe I didn't throw it out." Charles stood up on the

kitchen stool to reach the hairpin. "Somebody told her about our Chests, an' she saw the basket over at the store, an' she said for me to look there tonight and I'd find a dollar bill. And if I didn't want to take it for fixing her stove, I could say it was to pay for the cress."

"Did she take all that watercress too? Boy-y-y, that cousin of hers must be an awful eater. Did Horace find a rainbow, Charles?"

"Uh-huh. He's gone down Braeside with George."

"Down Braeside?" cried Mrs. Buckle, dipping a corner of the towel in a bowl of cool water and wiping her forehead with it. "I told Mr. Watson we'd keep to our own side of the County Road until he came back from Gananoque, and here every last one of you is running up and down that street as if you were as welcome as a day in May."

"But we are, Mother," Fan explained smugly. "We're getting acquainted fast and we've all been invited, now. Mr. Hooke likes Eddy. He even said that he didn't know how Braeside ever got along without the Buckles. That was after Eddy put Aunty Belle's bonnet with the green lilacs and the purple veil on his scarecrow. Captain Todd likes George an' me; Mrs. Mold likes Delia; probably Mrs. Witchit'll like Charles after he fixes her stove, an' he can have her. All we got to do now is to wait an' see how Horace makes out with his magician."

Mr. Liggard was on his knees weeding the petunias in

his garden, but he got up and moved toward the bench under the honeysuckle vine as soon as he heard the gate click and saw what was coming down the path.

"Well, sir, I thought something would show up from that storm last night," he roared. "Nelly!"

Mrs. Liggard appeared in the side door. "So you found a rainbow, dears?" she asked.

Horace held both hands behind his back and his thoughts, it was easily seen, were busy elsewhere. Sociability, if indulged in at all, was to be George's lot.

"Yes'm," said George blandly. "It wasn't a very big rainbow, but Mr. Liggard didn't say how big it had to be. This was just a teeny one in a raindrop that was hanging on a birch twig in the sunshine. But Horace was afraid to wait any longer for a big sky rainbow, in case it might not rain again while we were on the trailer, and he had something that he had to give to——"

"My magician," sighed Horace, unclasping his hands and bringing them to the fore. "Here's my story stick for you. His name is Impy."

"An' he loves it," George made haste to add. "Don't get the idea that Horace is trying to get rid of it because folks say, 'Don't be like Impy, Horace!' so much. He wouldn't give it to anybody but you, an' he wouldn't give it to you even, only he's sorry he stuck his tongue out so impolitely. Horace really is an I'm polite kid, you know. We all are. Have you got to know the story about the Impy stick, sir?"

"I'm afraid it will be necessary."

"All right. Only Horace isn't going to enjoy it the way he always has before he stuck his tongue out at you. Shall I begin now?"

"So you are the storyteller, eh?"

"Fan generally is, only she said never again about that old black duck. Shall I begin?"

"Please do."

Mrs. Liggard came down the steps and seated herself beside her husband on the bench under the honeysuckle vine while George got under way. "I'll have that stick, dear," she said in a low voice so as not to interrupt, "to hold up my white poppies."

"You hand that stick back to me," roared Mr. Liggard, as George finished. "That is my stick. I'm the magician around this house. Ask Horace, here, if you don't believe me."

"You a magician, Bert Liggard, oh my!"

"All right, just you wait till I fetch my handkerchief." He was gone no more than two minutes. When he returned he flourished the square of linen over little Horace's meek, golden head and rumbled, "Adabracadabra!"

Two brown objects tumbled to the grassy path and Horace was on them like a swallow on a gnat. "Bunnies!" he shrieked. "He said there'd be bunnies in his home if we found a rainbow, but he didn't say they'd be chocolate bunnies! One for you an' one for me, George. Hey-y-y, give the handkerchief a good squeeze, why don't you, sir."

"Why should I?"

"Fan an' Delia an' Charles an' Eddy an' Mother like chocolate bunnies too, I bet you."

Mr. Liggard drew Horace against his knee and rumpled his curls. "Gorry, but you're a little feller," he said.

"We're all littles," George explained pleasantly. "And we've all got yellow heads. Pa says it's a punishment on him for taking so much pleasure in fields of dandelions on sunny May mornings, but he's only fooling. He likes us to be littles."

"I wouldn't doubt it." Mr. Liggard suddenly twisted one of Horace's golden curls between his fingers, snatched the linen handkerchief aside, and a crisp new one dollar bill dropped to the sod. George's eyes popped, but Horace showed little interest. He simply stood against Mr. Liggard's knee and waited.

"Pick it up," ordered George, quivering with excitement. "You're the only one that hasn't done much for the Chests, only five cents' worth of weeding onions, and now a whole dollar."

"I'm afraid there are others in Braeside who haven't done even five cents' worth to help the war along," sighed Mrs. Liggard quietly. "We seemed to need a flock of children like all those Buckles to wake us up."

"Squeeze it," said Horace, waiting patiently.

Mr. Liggard flourished his handkerchief in the air. "Watch it," he shouted. "R-r-remember, the hand is quicker than the eye." And just then Mrs. Liggard

screamed and jumped to her feet, fumbling in her apron pocket wildly.

"Oh my goodness, look!" she cried. "I thought it was a bat or something that just banged against me. But it's —it's——"

"Golly, it's a whole bag of chocolate bunnies," shrilled little Horace, reaching for them. "That's the way! Come on, George, you can carry the Chest money, but I'll carry the bunnies." He reached up with one small hand, drew Mr. Liggard's wrinkled old cheek against his own velvety one, and smacked it damply. "Thank you, sir," he said. "I'm sorry I was Impy, and you can have my story stick forever and ever."

"Come and see us again, dears." Mrs. Liggard took the magician's handkerchief and tucked it inside her apron pocket as if it were quite an ordinary scrap of linen. "Come often," she urged. "Don't wait for another storm; we may have a dry summer, you know."

Mr. Liggard said nothing. He sat and rubbed his cheek for a full minute after the front gate clicked. And then he whispered proudly, "That little feller kissed me, Nelly. Golly, no little feller's kissed me since Bert's time, and our lad is a tough marine in the South Seas now."

Mrs. Liggard took his arm and together they walked among the lovely blossoms in the back garden. "Do you remember the time we had cactus dahlias against that fence, dear?" she asked. "And little Bert trampled them all down getting over the fence after Oliver Binns's great grandpappy? Children always trample gardens, don't they? They don't mean any harm by it. It's just that what they are doing seems of so much more importance."

"It is more important," Mr. Liggard agreed stoutly. "It's more important to grow a healthy, happy child, too, than any number of gardens. I wish those Buckles, the whole bunch of 'em, were living in Braeside."

"It would be nice, dear."

"Right across the street from us, at that," added Mr. Liggard, stoutly. Now that his opinion was changing it felt good to have it turn completely roundabout. "Little tenant house, kids, Vics, Roman chariot and all. When I think of how those children are working and planning every minute to help——"

"Why don't you do something about it, Bert?"

"Don't worry, I'm going to." Mr. Liggard stood still and stared at a robin till the poor thing let go of a worm that was half pulled and went off, piqued, in search of privacy. "I'm thinking," Mr. Liggard continued. "There's Todd. Now he wouldn't make any trouble if the Buckles should move onto Watson's vacant lot. Neither would Hooke. He's taken quite a fancy to the lad with the horse."

"Eddy."

"How in the world did you know his name, Nelly?"

Mrs. Liggard smiled. "It must be the magician's wife coming out in me," she said. "Penny Mold wouldn't mind having the children in Braeside, I know. But, there's Mrs. Witchit, and Tissy Binns, and, oh my goodness, there's Mr. Moom."

9. Piet

Eddy hadn't had any way of finding out where the Cliff-ton Center Pet Show would be held, but he was pretty sure that it would have to be in the school assembly room. No other place was big enough, now that Bandlo's circus tent was folded.

He slapped the reins along Mark's ridges and passed Shady Rest Cabins, Hamburgers, Antiques in a cloud of dust; he passed Downe's Drug Store in The Center so fast that a man who was going inside for a headache pill barely caught a glimpse of Nero's pink nightgown, but it was enough to make the man buy two pills instead of one and swallow them both on the spot. And so, in a shower of gravel, Eddy and Mark crossed the boys' playground of Lawrence School and came to a halt at the side entrance, commonly used by the lower grades.

"Whoa-a!" said Eddy. And Mark whoa-ed as nicely as any head scholar who has learned the toughest lesson in the book. Eddy climbed out of Nero by way of his slatted back, bumped his covered basket up and out to the ac-companiment of fierce, mysterious hissing, tied Mark to a paling around the corner of the building, and, returning to the side door, opened it. Professor Calmut blocked the passage.

This was not according to plan. The lady teachers of the lower grades made much of Professor Calmut, but to Eddy the man was a pickle and a bore. What Eddy didn't know was that to Professor Calmut he, himself, was simply another small boy bringing a basket, and Professor Calmut had handled too many baskets for his own good that day.

Ever since daybreak he had been moving benches and heavy tables and damp baskets this way and that for a decorating committee that couldn't agree; and when, at long last, the committee did come to some sort of an agreement it was upon a water scheme that had never been considered until that moment.

There it was, however. And so Professor Calmut drew on a pair of soft leather wading boots and went down to the river for reeds, cattails, and pickerel grass and he had just returned, dripping at all points, when, lifting a bench out of his way, he opened the side door and came face to face with Eddy Buckle.

It was the basket, however, that was Professor Calmut's last straw. He jostled the boy aside with the bench, kicked out under it at the basket, and succeeded in overturning it. Oliver Binns erupted and Oliver Binns was in no more of a mood for trifling than was Professor Calmut himself.

"Good heavens, help-p!" shrieked the professor, trying to bend over the bench to see what it was that was holding him by the toe under there. "Somebody help-p! There's a wildcat out here, he's bitten my foot to the bone. Get him, or this bench, off of me, somebody!"

The First Grade door opened and Miss Lettice came out. She had soft pink cheeks, merry brown eyes, and a wild rose in her hair, and of all the teachers in the Lawrence School, Miss Lettice was the one approved by all pupils of all grades.

"Hello, Eddy," she said gaily. And then, "What's all the excitement about a wildcat?"

"Grab his tail, haul him off," howled Professor Calmut fiercely. "Here I am, dying of lockjaw, probably, and you——"

"Lockjaw? You?" Miss Lettice giggled and drew a scrap of lace from her pocket. "Hardly, Timmy," she gasped, waving the kerchief before her nose. "Not with all the racket you are making. But it certainly does smell as if something was dying, or dead. Oh-h-h, what a gorgeous kitty, Eddy, is it yours?"

"Yes, ma'am. Just for today."

"What makes him smell so?"

"Sardines. They're leaking through."

"Pull him off. Pull him off!" roared Professor Calmut. But Miss Lettice said, "Hush, Timmy, I can't hear what Eddy Buckle is saying. What was it, dear?"

"I said nobody could pull Oliver off unless he wanted to let go," Eddy repeated, to Professor Calmut's greater distress. "He'll have to be tricked."

"Well, trick him, then."

"Yes, sir, I'm going to." Eddy removed a torn bit of oily paper from his blouse, smelled of it to see if it was still potent, decided that it was, and wafted it temptingly under Mr. Binns's twitching nose. Oliver forsook the wading boot, to pounce upon the more savory tidbit. And was neatly trapped as Eddy clapped the covered basket over him, up-ended it, and fastened the hasp. "Such a cat," he said. "So full of sardines that they leak through, and yet he'll jump to chew the paper they were wrapped up in. Where do I take him now, Miss Lettice?"

"Throw him in the river," advised Professor Calmut warmly. But Eddy ignored Professor Calmut.

"Where are the rest of the choice pets?" he asked.

Miss Lettice sat down on Professor Calmut's bench. "The rest of the choice pets?" she gasped. "Are all you Buckles bringing baskets of——"

A wintry smile lifted the corners of Eddy's mouth for a mere instant. "Of course not," he replied. "Their Vics wouldn't stand a chance against mine."

"Vics? Do you mean that you are earning money for our Chests with that monstrous cat, Eddy dear?"

"Yes, ma'am. I stuffed him with fish to make him fatter and shinier."

"But, Eddy, why did you bring him here to our show?"

Eddy stooped over the basket and Professor Calmut, watching his every move, shouted a stern warning. "Don't you open that trap, son."

Eddy went about his business, undisturbed. He lifted the cover barely far enough to allow for the entrance of his small, groping fist and, feeling the oily paper crumpled in a corner of Oliver's mouth, he removed it coolly while Miss Lettice fanned herself first with her scrap of lace and later, finding that insufficient, with Professor Calmut's handkerchief.

"Here you are," said Eddy, spreading what was left of the paper on the farthest corner of the bench. "This'll explain it. Fan found it under Captain Todd's hedge and he wrote an invitation on one side of it, but I kept the other side to think about."

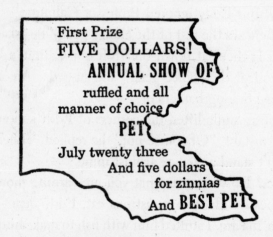

"Why, that's a handbill about our show, Eddy," said Miss Lettice, still puzzled.

"Sure it is. 'The Annual Show of' something or other. Oliver chewed that corner off, I guess. Here's what I want, though, see? 'All Manner of Choice Pet.' And down here it says, 'Five Dollars for the Best Pet.' I don't see how anybody could have a choicer pet than Oliver, if he only behaves himself. Of course he might get to raising cain, but if he does I've got another sardine in my pants pocket that he doesn't know anything about, yet. That'll make him sit up and mind his manners, I bet you."

Professor Calmut sat down on the bench beside Miss Lettice and shouted with laughter until Miss Lettice put her hand on his knee and ordered him to stop at once. "This is no laughing matter, Timmy," she said. "Not since Oliver has given up thinking you were a sardine. This is going to be pretty sad for somebody maybe."

And then, leaning forward and speaking slowly, she tried to explain to Eddy that the handbill which he had saved and studied so carefully was not a notice of any pet show at all, but of the Annual Cliffton Center Flower Show. And the prize was for the best petunia. An exhibit of all manner of choice petunias and zinnias. It took Eddy some time to get it, but he finally did.

"Petunias?" he wailed. "For gosh sakes!"

"Pet, pet, petunias!" spluttered Professor Calmut, pushing Miss Lettice's hand away from his mouth to say it. "He came all the way from wherever he came from, lugging a thousand pounds of wildcat to a petunia show. Oh-h, I hope I never forget this, and I don't think I will!"

Five women bustled nearer, rustling bits of paper and whispering among themselves importantly; they smiled brightly upon Professor Calmut and Miss Lettice and then disappeared inside the First Grade room. Miss Lettice sprang to her feet.

"Mrs. Gorse and her committee of judges, Timmy," she warned. "They're meeting for last minute instructions before looking over the exhibits. Bring that basket, and you come too, Eddy."

Professor Calmut hesitated. "You want me to bring that 'petunia'? Where?"

"Into the First Grade room; hurry up before the committee is too busy to listen to us."

Mrs. Gorse turned her head and smiled again, but not so brightly, as the door opened. "Please, dear Mrs. Gorse, I won't take more than a minute of your valuable time," Miss Lettice promised sweetly. "But I do want you to meet Eddy Buckle; you remember the Buckles? The best war workers in the whole school. You know what they have brought to the Chests of Cheer."

"I certainly do, my dear. Enthusiastic little souls, kind little creatures." Mrs. Gorse appeared about ready to boil over. "So this is Eddy? Well, well! And is he going in for better gardening? A whole basketful of petunias, eh?"

Miss Lettice explained Eddy's mistake in a few words and it took Mrs. Gorse longer to get it than it had Eddy. However, with the help of Professor Calmut and the other four ladies, she began to have an inkling of what was expected of her, at last, and was pretty gracious about it.

"Dear me, a pet to a petunia show," she tinkled merrily. "Well, of course he shall have a prize. We want to do all we can to keep the spirit of helpfulness alive among the dear, dear children. And I am very sure nobody will object, nobody here, since we know all the circumstances and since I happen, very fortunately, to have an extra blue ribbon in my portfolio." She stooped and looped the blue ribbon about the handle of the covered basket. "There," she said, dusting her fingers daintily. "A first prize for the Buckle's best pet."

The four ladies tittered and whispered, nodded to each other approvingly, and rustled their papers. Eddy made no sign of withdrawal. Even a born gentleman can take only so much and no more humiliation in silence, it seems, and Eddy was preparing to speak.

"Pinhooks!" he said. "War kids can't eat ribbon!"

Mrs. Gorse fell back. The four ladies ceased murmuring and their papers were stilled. And at just that moment the covered basket threatened to explode with a mighty hiss-ss-ssssss.

"Why-y!" said Mrs. Gorse, with a kind of smacking gasp.

"War kids eat bacon," Eddy came to the point at once. "Five dollars would buy a lot of bacon. You can't buy anything with a blue ribbon."

"You surely don't mean that you expect the grand prize for bringing a cat to our flower show?" Mrs. Gorse could lift her voice too upon occasion. "Well, I never!"

"Well, I have, if you know what I mean," shouted Professor Calmut, unable, once more, to control his merriment. "I can believe this thing, and I have seen the cat, and unless you ladies want to see it, and smell it, you'd better believe, too, that Eddy Buckle needs five dollars for his war Chests and means to have it. If I am any judge, I should say that three minutes of arguing the matter would be plenty of time for the cat to break loose and start lunching on the toes around here. So I, for one, would urge haste." He opened his purse and extracted a crisp, new, five dollar bill. "Mr. Buckle," he said, "may I have the honor of presenting Mr. Binns, through you, with a grand prize as being the best pet of this show?"

Eddy accepted the five dollar bill calmly. The five lady judges were anything but calm, however, when they saw him bend above the basket. They gasped, with quite lady-like little puffs to be sure, but still strong enough to make a decided draft around teacher's desk.

"Don't open your basket, Eddy," said Mrs. Gorse. "I wouldn't."

"I've got to," was the cold reply. "You heard him. He presented the grand prize to Oliver. I've got to put it in his locket. Probably when Miss Binns hears about it, she'll make him give it to the Chests; if she doesn't her old cat'll wish she had."

Eddy lifted the basket cover a crack and Mrs. Gorse screamed. Eddy was bored. "Well, stand back then," he advised sharply. "Golly, it's only sardines. But if I can't open his locket without taking the cover way off, I'll have to do it and Oliver's likely to come out. And if he does,

he'll jump on the first thing he sees, an' my gosh, there
he goes!"

Mrs. Gorse happened to be the first thing that Oliver
saw as he burst from his prison, but Mrs. Gorse had her
eyes open, too. She was leaning against the door to the
Second Grade room and just as Oliver leaped for her she
opened the door and closed it with a bang, and in that
second of time she freed the First Grade room of two
beings who had no part in a flower show, because Eddy
followed Mr. Binns like his own black shadow into the
Second Grade room.

It was murky in the Second Grade room. Books and
papers and unwanted odds and ends from the flower show,
cast-off containers, hollyhock stalks, unsightly evergreen
boughs that had been refused by the decorators, and
bunches of dripping reeds and rushes were piled high on
the window sills, shutting out most of the light. And
across one corner of the room were all the pine tables,
from the assembly room. The blackboards were fuzzy with
the ghosts of past lessons. It was not an attractive place
to be caught in, alone. Knowing that an enraged Oliver
Binns was lurking somewhere in the shadows made the
room no cosier. Eddy dug deeply into his pants pocket,
closed his fingers on the spare sardine, and felt better.

"Oliver," he quavered. "Here y'are, Oliver. I bet I know
where you are."

There being no response, Eddy waved the sardine this
way and that. "Come and get it, Oliver," he piped.

Eddy began to feel nervous. After all, he told himself, Oliver Binns had to be in that room. There was only one corner that held possible secrets. He dropped to his knees and crept behind the tottering pile of pine tables, benches, stools, desks and chairs that had been cleared from the assembly room, and so, in the dusk and dust of that far corner, came face to face with a strange boy.

"Ullo," whispered the stranger. "Fancy this spot being so public like. The door opens and whoosh, in comes a cat as if he knew all about this cave. And now you. I'd have been safer behind the boughs by the window, I'm thinking."

"Safer from what?" asked Eddy. But without waiting for an answer he tossed a second question into the silence. "Did you grab my cat?"

"I didn't need to; come closer and look. Poor, gorgeous puss. He was in need of a bit of a rest." Eddy's eyes were accustomed somewhat to the dusk in the cave by this time; enough, anyway, to reveal Mr. Binns's presence in all his shameful languor. "Stretched out right across my knees, he did," said the boy. "Begging for a bit of scratching behind the ears and a spot of peaceful slumber."

"Rest, slumber—pinhooks!" said Eddy Buckle wearily. "That cat had all the chance in the world to be a grand prize. I just about broke my bank buying sardines for him. But what does he do? Acts up like a weed in a—well, like a hunk of crabgrass in a petunia show, if you can imagine it. Coarse, that's what he is."

"He smells grand though. Fishy like."

Eddy stared at the lean, pale face before him. "Are you hungry, boy?" he asked.

"Who isn't hungry for kippers and potatoes fried in grease? If all your cat did was to eat sardines——"

"He did plenty more than that. He almost chewed a man's toe off, and what man was it, I ask you? Nobody. Only the man that's going to teach me arithmetic next year. And then, just as soon as I clicked his prize money into his locket, he tried to give me the slip and made off with it. Went for Mrs. Gorse like a sky rocket."

"Gar! I wouldn't blame him too much for that."

"What's your name, boy?" asked Eddy.

"Piet. What's yours?"

"Eddy Buckle. Are you visitin' somebody here in The Center?"

"Not half! Mrs. Gorse took us off the committee's hands, so she said."

"Mrs. Gorse?"

"Not so loud, Eddy. That one has ears like a redbreast and eyes like a kestrel. She's got a liver, too, and that's bad."

"Why is it?" asked Eddy, bewildered.

"Because it keeps her from eating fried fish, and it gets worse when children sob. And of course Ol' Love has to sob most of the time, now, worrying about Mom and—"

A muffled sob from somewhere in the gloom beyond cut

Piet's explanation short and startled Eddy backward on his heels. Piet groped behind his back and took a firm grasp on something. "There, there, Ol' Love," he begged, "hold it."

Eddy's eyes popped and he retreated farther toward the Second Grade room's larger, less occupied spaces as Piet brought to light a very damp, very grubby lass and a most unsavory bundle of rags. The girl wiped her dripping eyes on the rags, muffled her sobs in it, and cuddled the bundle for comfort into the curve of her small neck.

"This here is Ol' Love," said Piet simply. "Mrs. Gorse insists upon calling her Rosalove, and of course that is what her tag says, but Mom and I call her—there, there, Ol' Love, hold it."

"Is your mom dead?" asked Eddy, sympathetically.

"Dead? No! Of course she isn't." Piet was fiercely upset at the question. "She's lost for a time. That's all. Or maybe it is that Ol' Love and I are lost. Anyway, we're separated for a bit, since we were bombed out."

"Bombed!" Eddy started. "Are you a war kid, Piet?"

Piet considered the question, but gave it up. "I probably don't understand your meaning," he said.

"Were you over where the war is?"

"Oh quite. Our farm was bombed—in Dover, you know. And then we were bombed out of London. So then it was decided to send as many children as possible away from the city and Mom made up her mind to bring Ol' Love and me to our aunty in the States. We came with

a whole shipload of children; Mom was in charge of the little ones. Our Mom is very good at cuddling little children when they are frightened."

"So's mine," said Eddy, waiting for Ol' Love to dry her tears.

"So then," Piet continued, "we were bombed out of our ship."

"Golly! They were right after you, weren't they?" Eddy doubled his small fist against an unseen and most unfair enemy, but Piet merely drew his soggy little sister closer within his sheltering arm and patted her unkempt head.

"They were kind enough to bomb us within sight of your shores, anyway." Piet gave the enemy that much credit. "Sailor Bob was pretty certain that all the lifeboats and rafts would drift safely to land, somewhere. The only trouble was that Mom, being in charge of the very little ones you see, was put in one boat, and Ol' Love and I in quite a different craft under Sailor Bob's care. We would have preferred being together during the whole journey. There, there, Ol' Love, take Skipper and have a wipe. This here," Piet held up the bundle of sour rags that Rosalove had been cuddling in the curve of her neck, "this here is Skipper," he said. "Sailor Bob made him out of a handful of waste and a portion of a torn sail. He painted the eyes and nose and whiskers and cap from a bucket of black he was using around the engines and he told Ol' Love he looked more like the Skipper than his own likeness in a mirror. 'Twas a bit of cheer for Ol' Love. She wouldn't leave the bombed ship until she had Skipper tucked under her chin."

Eddy glanced at Skipper without enthusiasm. He felt that something was expected of him, but he didn't know what. All he could think of to say was that Skipper was pretty wet, and Piet agreed to that. "Mrs. Gorse was always remarking the same thing," he nodded, rather unhappily. "Skipper was bad for her liver, too. She wanted to boil him up in a copper of suds, but Ol' Love fought that one out with her. When Mom comes she'll give Skipper a rare going-over."

A tremendous thought suddenly pitched Eddy forward, almost nose to nose with the strangers. "Piet, are you an' Ol' Love Mr. Watson's family? Are you, Piet?"

"Mr. Watson? Never heard the name."

Eddy was disappointed. "Pinhooks, I was hoping you were," he sighed. "Mr. Watson has gone to Gananoque to get a family of war kids, an' their ship was bombed, an' he's hanging around there until they float ashore."

"Yes? Another shipload, probably. Oh, too bad, too bad. I hope they make it safely as we did. Ol' Love and I have our own family, though, Eddy. We're going to our aunty's place in Cliffton Center. Mom fastened a tag with the name on it around our necks. Cliffton Center, I was to remember that town."

"You got here all right, then. This is Cliffton Center where we are now, Piet."

"So Mrs. Gorse said. Only she doesn't seem to be able

to locate our aunty. Mrs. Gorse explained to us that she
was on a committee to meet and look out for the children
that were coming on our boat, but when she heard that
some of us had floated ashore at quite an unexpected
place, she offered to take charge of us, because it was
nearer than Gan—Gan——"

"Gananoque."

"That's it. All the children were supposed to be brought
to Gan—whatever that place is, by motors, but we, being
the first to land, were carried to Riverhead. And that's
where Mrs. Gorse picked us up. As soon as she saw
'Cliffton Center' on our tags she said she would take us
right off the committee's hands and we could stay with
her overnight, and join out aunty in the morning. We've
been with her two days now, and she doesn't know what to
do with us. It's making her liver very bad."

"What is? I don't get it. Doesn't she like company?"

"Well, not us, I should think. She can't find our aunty
in Cliffton Center and she's beginning to worry about
whether we have an aunty or not. Of course we have, you
know, but she says she's been mistaken about so many
things in this war that one aunty more or less wouldn't
surprise her any. You don't happen to know a lady by
the name of Penelope Paxton, do you?"

Eddy didn't. And the gloom in the Second Grade room
deepened. "Gar," sighed Piet. "It was too much to hope
for. Well, Mrs. Gorse said that as a last resort she was
going to take us to a flower show today where everybody

for miles around would be, and stand us up on a table, and ask the folks if anybody had ever heard of our Aunty Penelope. Ol' Love began to quiver at that, she's timid with strangers, and I told her to hold it, that I would find some way to make a dash for it, and I did. Only there doesn't seem to be any way out of this room except through that door. And Mrs. Gorse is meeting with her ladies in there."

"You think so." Eddy grinned. "But I was brought up in this school. There's a coat room door behind those old screens; and if the outside door in there is locked, why, there are two windows where we can drop right into the boys' playground. I know the way all over this place Where are you going after you get out of here?"

Silence, as well as gloom, deepened in the Second Grade room. No one spoke until Eddy said, "Our house is kind of what you might call traveling just now. We have to watch out not to step into the dishes that are stacked up along the walls, but nobody's got a liver. How would you like to come along home with me?"

There was a sudden boiling among the stacked tables, desks, stools, and benches. "Hold it, hold it, Ol' Love!" begged Piet, both hands clutched to a green plaid skirt. "An' you hold it too, you ol' doublecrosser," hissed Eddy, succeeding through a bit of pure luck in getting a firm grip on Mr. Binns's locket. "Don't think you're going to get away with that five dollar bill."

"I'd slap him down good," he added in an aside to Piet

after the worst of the storm was over. "That is, if Ol' Love hadn't stepped on his tail. An' if," he added still further, "I could. Those sardines have made him awful strong. I've got to get him back in his basket."

"Wouldn't he follow on?"

"Trust that cat on the loose with five dollars in his locket?" Eddy's expression showed clearly where he stood on that issue. "His basket is in there with Mrs. Gorse."

"Then we won't have it. I'll carry him in my arms," said Piet firmly. "He won't escape me, I promise you. Is it far to your home?"

"Oh, down the road a bit, beside a swale. It's not a real 'home' yet, you know. Not until Mr. Watson gets back from Gananoque and does something about it. I don't know if you could hold Oliver down in Nero."

"Nero? Who would that be?"

"That's my cart. I've got a horse, Mark, and a cart outside here."

"Then let's go promptly, shall we? I'll carry the puss, and you, Ol' Love, tuck Skipper under your arm and follow on. Right?"

It was, it seemed, perfectly right with Rosalove. She darted ahead of everybody, found the door behind the screen, and discovered that it was unlocked. As an added bit of luck, the covered basket was seen to be just outside where Miss Lettice had put it for an airing. It was only necessary for Eddy to drop the spare sardine inside to make Oliver a prisoner once more. And after one slap of the reins across his ridgy back, Mark left the Cliffton Center Petunia Show as he had come, in a spatter and shower of gravel.

Mark, moreover, kept moving right along at the same high rate of speed until he had reached the little tenant house and swerved into the swale. He knew as well as the next one when he was headed for home and a bucketful of boiled potato parings, and he brought up against Mr. Watson's trailer with a hopeful bang.

The little tenant house began to buzz like a disturbed beehive. Golden heads blossomed at the windows and both door openings, and then children started dropping from everywhere to the trailer where they stood in a row, looking downward into Nero.

Piet stood up. "Is this—is this it, Eddy?" he asked.

Eddy nodded.

"Why, it's a proper house!" Piet's approval was hearty and unstinted. "It's grand. Eh, Ol' Love?"

"Potatoes frying in grease, and fish," sighed Rosalove. But it was Fan who really drew her forth from behind the basket for a closer view, leaving Skipper in a damp, neglected heap where he fell. "There's a little girl, Piet," she whispered.

And at the same moment Fan, who never whispered, shrilled at the top of her lungs, "Moth-er-r, here's Eddy. An' he's got a boy an' an awful white little girl with him."

Mrs. Buckle slid through the doorway and, reaching

downward, drew Rosalove out of Nero. "Well, well," she said. "Well, well, well, well!"

"They're war kids," Eddy explained. "They don't know it, but they are. I found 'em at—hey-y-y, Mother, what do you know. I took Oliver Binns to a pet show and it was a petunia show. Gosh! You never saw anything like how the people took on about him 'cause he smelled so strong."

"I bet he didn't smell no stronger than petunias," piped Fan indignantly. "What made you take that old cat to see the flowers, Eddy?"

Eddy could hardly bear such a thought. "I took him to earn five dollars for the Chests," he replied with cold dignity.

"That old black Vaughn? How could he?"

"Well, he did, that's all. He won the first prize."

"Where's the money? I wouldn't believe it even if——"

"You will just as soon as I open his locket."

"Tell us about these other two prizes." Mrs. Buckle hugged Rosalove and chuckled merrily. "How did you get them, Eddy?"

The uproar as the Buckles surged up the orange boxes and into the kitchen was terrific. "Boy-y-y, the Vics that Eddy brings home when he gets around to it," piped Fan. "Where's her mother, Eddy?"

"Golly, now you've done it, Fan Buckle." Eddy was shocked. "Hold it, Ol' Love," he begged.

It may be that Rosalove hadn't heard. It might be, that she, too, was slightly shocked at her first meeting with all those Buckles after visiting for two days with the Gorses. Whatever the reason, Rosalove was holding it serenely. She accepted a chocolate bunny from little Horace without even noticing that it was minus a head; she approved gravely when George, who had found Skipper, saluted the wreck with a hoarse, "Ahoy-y-y, mate!" But as soon as she discovered that it was Delia who was turning fish in the skillet, her eyes never wavered from Delia and the stove.

"She's hungry for fish an' fried potatoes," Eddy whispered in his mother's ear. His mother, he knew, could hear any whisper no matter how loud the uproar about her. "Piet an' Ol' Love were on that boat that Mr. Hooke told us about. The one that Mr. Watson went to meet, but it was bombed, you know. You remember what the paper said about it?"

Mrs. Buckle nodded. "It said the poor people were on rafts, or lifeboats."

"Sure. They'll float in to land somewhere. But they got separated, don't you see? These two were to be taken to their Aunty Penelope in The Center. Only Mrs. Gorse couldn't find her an' Mrs. Gorse doesn't like kids, you know, an' she got a liver every time Ol' Love sobbed for her mom. I told Piet an' Ol' Love they could stay with us until Mr. Watson found their mom in Gananoque. He'll know how to bring together those who have been separated, I told Piet."

"Well, he won't." Fan, it seemed, could catch a whisper as well as the next one. "It's the angels who are going to do that. Mother told us to ask them in our prayers last night and we all did. Now don't you bother 'em, Eddy Buckle. Just let 'em do their job; Mr. Watson'll have plenty to attend to when he comes back. Has—what's her name, Eddy?"

"Rosalove. But folks who love her call her Ol' Love. Piet an' I do."

"Has Ol' Love got to wear that dirty old green dress all the time, Mother?"

Every Buckle eye in the kitchen stared at Fan reproachfully. Fan, however, was mild and entirely affable. " 'Cause if she doesn't have to," she added delicately, "she could have my best pink sunsuit. She'd look like a cunning little doll in that, with her hair washed an' tied with a pink bow. You like pinky things too, don't you, Ol' Love?"

Rosalove did, judging by her shining eyes, but it was Piet who answered for her. "Ol' Love had plenty of frocks in our luggage box in the ship that was bombed and went bottoms up," he said proudly. "Frocks of all colors except green. Green was Mrs. Gorse's choice. Very neat she used to look all the time."

"I bet she did, lovey." Mrs. Buckle rumpled the soft brown curls at her knee lovingly. "And it might be that Fan's idea is just the one. Hold back that fish for ten minutes, Delia, and fill the basin at the sink with hot water."

"You can use all you want to of my pink soap, Ol' Love." Fan ran to get it. And found something else very precious in her treasure box. "And you can have this beautiful, beautiful pink bow for your hair. Miss Lettice made it for me last Christmas 'cause I worked so hard for her Chests."

The boys dropped to the swale to feed Mark while the scrubbing was going on, but what they saw on the kitchen stool when Delia called them back brought them up short on the doorsill.

"Gar," said Piet, not even trying to hide his pride. "A rare beauty, Ol' Love. What?"

"An' just smell of her," Fan invited with still greater pride. "That's my pink soap that makes her smell like roses. Push over, George," she added, busy with the seating arrangements at the table. "Ol' Love is going to sit next to me. I've got to see that she doesn't eat too much fish an' potatoes, 'cause we've got tapioca pudding an' roz'b'ries an' whipped cream after that. Boy-y-y, I hope that Mrs. Gorse doesn't ever find out that Ol' Love an' Piet are in Braeside."

Clattering knives, forks, and spoons fell silent at once; the skillet of fish tottered and sputtered under Delia's hand on the stove; the alphabet lifted stricken eyes to Mrs. Buckle.

"Of course Mrs. Gorse must know that the children are in Braeside; the things you think of, Fan sweety," she said calmly, beginning to dish up the browned potatoes. "As soon as we have finished eating I'll go over to the store and use Mr. Hanley's phone to tell her, myself. We don't want her worrying too much about the children, you know."

"She won't worry." Piet sighed over the memory of the last few days. "Her liver might be much better with us gone."

"Just the same, deary, she's responsible to the committee for you. I'll tell her that the Buckles will take over that job from now on. Until Mr. Watson gets back from Gananoque, anyway. He'll know what to do. Likely he'll find your aunty right away. You just eat all the fish you can hold, my pets, and trust to Mr. Watson."

10. Mr. Moom Becomes a Regular Customer

CHARLES chased the last crimson berry through the last puddle of cream, captured it, and announced that he was returning to Mrs. Witchit's house that afternoon, in response to a most pressing invitation.

"What's wrong with her stove now, deary?" asked Mrs. Buckle.

"Nothing. She just likes to have me around the place. She says I'm like her own little boy when he was my age. She's going to make me some raisin cookies. And she's awfully ashamed of hollering to Mr. Moom about us that day when we first moved down the road. She's a very nice lady, Mother."

"So is Mrs. Mold a nice lady," said Delia, to the surprise of everybody. "Mother, do you know it is Mrs. Mold who has been buying Julia's egg off the basket in the store. She says the Buckles have shown her how she can have some little part in helping the sufferers from this war and maybe she'll pay fifty cents for every egg after this. She says each time she takes Julia's egg out of the store she feels that she has done something to make her sister a little happier."

"Her sister, deary? Who is that?"

"I don't know. Somebody who lives over where the war is. Mrs. Mold thinks she must have been bombed to bits because she hasn't heard from her for so long, but I told her not to worry. I told her that we were all praying to the good angels to bring together those who have become separated an' it wouldn't surprise me at all to see her sister come walking right into Braeside any day now."

Fan started to her feet. "Hey-y, you go right over to her house and tell her that all that praying isn't for *her* sister, Delia Buckle," she cried. She was incensed at such a trick. "That praying is going to be for Ol' Love's mom. First thing you know you'll be getting the angels all mixed up."

"No fear, sweety. The angels know what's what." Mrs. Buckle calmed the rising storm with a nod and chuckle. "We could maybe spare a prayer or two for Mrs. Mold's sister, at that."

"I'm going to." said Delia boldly. "I told Mrs. Mold I would. And what do you think she said? She said, 'God bless all those Buckles.' Just like that. She really did. The way she said, 'All those Buckles,' didn't sound like the way Mr. Jole said it either, when he wouldn't rent us a house, not a bit. I'm going over to her house this afternoon to help her trim the little white roses. She invited me to come."

"Next?" asked Mrs. Buckle gaily. "After being alone most of the time since we moved alongside this swale, it'll seem good to have a pair of twins under foot again, anyway."

"You won't have me," George announced at once. "Captain Todd invited me to help him calk THE MOLLY."

"An' you won't have me under foot." Fan pushed away from the table and shook Katy and Lulu out of the scrub bucket. "I'm going to take this out under the elderberries an' fill it with soap flakes an' hot water an' give Skipper a sudsing."

Piet choked. "Now you've done it again, lass," he groaned.

Rosalove, however, made no move to "have it out" with Fan as she had with Mrs. Gorse. After her first mouthful of fish and potatoes she had tucked the dirty bundle of rags behind her back and now, hauling it forth, she handed it to Fan with complete indifference. Rosalove was

in no further need of Skipper's comforting, if Piet had but known it.

"He'll be 'most as handsome as Captain Todd, I bet you, when he's cleaned an' hung on an elderberry twig to dry," said Fan, accepting the unpleasant object with the tips of her fingers and pulling Rosalove forward so that she could dust the back of the bright little sunsuit. "Golly, it's a wonder he didn't stain you all up. Hey-y-y, listen to Vaughn howl, Eddy."

"He knows there's eating going on."

"What you going to do with him? Buy him some more sardines?"

"Not me. I'm going to take him home and see what Miss Binns does about that prize money."

"Can you hold that cat down an' open his locket when he's mad as that?" Fan dropped Skipper onto a stool and scooped Katy and Lulu back into the scrub bucket. "Don't open that basket around here, Eddy!" she warned. "Not until you get him way down Braeside. Only how you're going to explain to Miss Binns when you do get down there about walking right into her garden without an invitation——"

"Pinhooks! She'll be glad enough to get her old cat back."

"You'll need help in managing the poor lad once his basket is opened," said Piet, rising from his stool. "I'll go along, Eddy."

Rosalove slipped from her stool and snuggled her little

fist inside Piet's. He patted it gently. "Of course you shall go with me, if you so wish, Ol' Love," he assured her. "We'll stick together, I promise you, until Mom has joined us."

Fan seated herself on the edge of the scrub bucket and took issue with Piet. "You can't go down Braeside with Piet, Ol' Love," she said. "I don't even believe Piet can go."

"Why not then?" asked Piet, puzzled.

" 'Cause the folks down there don't like children."

"What's their reason?"

"Oh-h, they're pretty old, you know. And they haven't got any little children around the place for samples. Though if they had a lad like Sam Cooter living there I wouldn't blame 'em. He is the kind that carries green snakes in his pocket. He had Eddy's job at Bandlo's."

"But this Sam chap doesn't live there?"

"No. I wouldn't be surprised if they have heard about him, though. Anyway, they think all children are diggers and trampers."

"Diggers? Trampers?"

"Around their hollyhock roots and over their petunias. Bad for their gardens, don't you see, like puppies and cats. Of course Oliver Binns lives there, and he's puh-len-ty! Mother told us that we must not go down Braeside unless we were invited."

"And so you haven't been down the lane, eh?"

"Law me, we just about live there." Fan counted off

the Buckles on her small fingers with a smug grin. "There's George an' me, we had a written invitation from Captain Todd. We were the first of all. Then, I bet you, the folks saw that we wouldn't harm their gardens, 'cause Mrs. Mold invited Delia an' Mr. Liggard——"

"He's my magician," Horace interrupted happily.

"Well, whatever he is, he lives next to the last house on that side of the street. Mr. Moom lives in the last house but he has strictly invited *nobody* to visit him, you bet you! That old black cat out there lives across the street from Mr. Moom an' if Eddy thinks it's an invitation just to take him back home to Miss Binns, all right. I wouldn't go with him for anything. Of course the man who lives next to her, Mr. Hooke, did invite Eddy. And he gave him a job, too."

"An' that makes me think," Eddy interrupted quickly, "it's time I was getting around to that job. We'll put a rake an' broom in Nero with the covered basket an' Ol' Love."

"An' shovel all that scratchy old trash on top of Ol' Love?"

"Trash? On Ol' Love?" Piet was considerably set back, but Eddy motioned him toward the doorway and Rosalove followed like their shadow.

"We won't hurt her," Eddy explained when they were down in the swale. "You see, I've got the job of keeping Braeside clean of hedge clippings and such, down as far as Mr. Moom's place. He's no customer of mine, Piet.

I'll be earning quite a pile of money for the Chests of Cheer, for the poor people over where the war is, once I begin this work. I haven't turned in so much up to now, but I will with that cat's prize money (if I get it) an' this regular job."

"Can you do that all alone, Eddy?" Piet turned and looked down Braeside. "Quite an undertaking, I should think."

"I've got to. I spent all the money in my bank on Mark an' Nero so I could go really out on war work in a big way. I don't mind telling you," he confessed under his breath, "that I didn't know it would be quite so big. I'll swing it, though."

"Won't some of the others help?"

"Oh-h, they've all got their own businesses to look after. Charles is the only one big enough anyway, and he's got Imogene and Mrs. Witchit on his hands."

"If I could be of any service, old chap."

Eddy was dazzled by the offer. It was the solution of all his private worries. With Piet and himself to rake and toss the greenstuff inside Nero, and with Rosalove to trample it down and keep it from oozing out through the slats, the job was as good as started right that minute.

"Golly," he said, "I'll make you my partner, Piet. You'll get half of what I make and I don't mind telling you what I make isn't chicken feed. Every person in Braeside will be a regular customer after Mr. Hooke sees them about it, except Mr. Moom. Six houses and a vacant lot to keep raked up. Mr. Watson owns the vacant lot and I know he'll be a regular customer. You'll get close to two dollars a week, 'cause there'll be weeding and other odd jobs turn up."

"Two dollars? Each week, Eddy?"

"Sure. Cash payment, too. That's the way I do business."

"Gar." The future was almost too bright. There must be a shadow across it somewhere. Piet found it. "I would be expected to contribute my earnings to that—what was the name of that container, now?"

"The Chests of Cheer. Of course you'd be expected to help with it. You'd want to, wouldn't you?"

"Why certainly, old chap. Only for the moment I was hopeful of putting a bit of cash aside for Mom, just to get her started like."

"Started?" Eddy was puzzled. "Started where?" he asked. It didn't seem to him just the thing for Piet's mom to pop off somewhere else the moment she found her family. "I thought you were all going to live in Cliffton Center with your aunty."

"Of course, Eddy. But there will be a living to be earned for the three of us, until I am old enough to take over. Climb the slats, Ol' Love, and snuggle down behind the basket and puss. Our father," he continued when he and Eddy were alone and busy with Mark's rope, "our father has not yet returned from Dunkirk. He may be lost forever, or he may have been captured by the enemy and will join us later. We cannot be sure about this, but it is not a matter for weeping. We do not speak of him often before Ol' Love, but even if we did she would not sob. We all wear our pride in our father, as Mom bids us, with heads held high."

"Gosh!" said Eddy. And then again, "Gosh!"

"Our mom is a very fine seamstress," Piet continued, "and it was her plan to make a living for us with her needle while waiting for our father to return, or for me to grow up. It would ease her mind to find a bit of ready cash waiting for her in the States."

"Well, why shouldn't she?" said Eddy, rising to the occasion. "I guess there could be more war Chests than just the ones Miss Lettice fills. Now, say I put my cash into the Chests of Cheer, and you put yours into a 'Mom Chest.' And a 'Father Chest,' too! Golly, Piet, you'll have two Chests. Your father'll want a little something to get started on if, I mean when, he comes back from Dunkirk. We'd better get busy, do you know it?"

Mark and Nero heaved out of the swale and across the County Road.

"Do we begin with the corner house?" asked Piet.

"We don't begin anywhere until we take this cat home," Eddy reminded him firmly. "There's a five dollar bill in that cat's locket that's got to be fought for."

The ridgy horse and the startling cart trundled on down Braeside. In front of Mr. Hooke's house, Eddy said, "Whoa-a!" And then, turning to Piet, he asked, "What was it that you said your mom was good at earning a living at?"

Strangely enough, Piet understood the question. "Why, sewing," he replied. "Mom is a very fine seamstress. She was taught by the good Sisters in a convent near Rheims when a lass. Do you think the Braeside folks might be in need of a good seamstress, Eddy?"

Eddy positively didn't know. "I'll have to ask Mr. Hooke about it," he said. "He's my best Braeside friend and there he comes now."

"Ahoy, Eddy," shouted Mr. Hooke, trotting up from the back garden where he had been grubbing around the leeks. "I saw all the neighbors about that job for you and they all signed up at fifty cents per week with the exception of Mr. Moom." Mr. Hooke stopped a moment to catch his breath and fumble through his pockets for his spectacles. Having found them, he hung them across his nose and continued. "Moom is pretty crotchety about the idea of a Roman chariot gathering up his clippings. Bless my soul, is that another Buckle, Eddy?"

"No, sir. This is Piet. Could you use a very fine seamstress in Braeside, sir?"

"A what? You aren't planning to take on any more war work, are you, Eddy?"

"Yes, sir. It beats all how much of it there is to do."

"Doesn't it? But just what kind of seamstressing are you fitted to handle?"

"Golly, not me." Eddy was shocked at the mistake. "It's

for Piet's mom." And then, after Piet's story had been told in a few words, Eddy allowed Mr. Hooke to draw near and shake hands with Piet and also, since he knew that Ol' Love had been listening to the whole conversation and would understand, he invited Mr. Hooke to have a look inside Nero and shake hands with Ol' Love. After that Mr. Hooke took off his spectacles, wiped them on his blouse, and rubbed his eyes with the back of his hand.

"You wouldn't be acquainted with my Aunty Penelope Paxton, would you, sir?" asked Piet.

Mr. Hooke wiped his eyes again on the back of his other hand. "Sorry, lad, never heard of the lady," he said. And then, to Eddy, "About that seamstress business, though. I'll have another call around the block before sunset and put the matter right up to the neighbors. As for the Hookes, I can tell you this minute they are in desperate need of a sewing woman. I just ripped a button off my shirt, and there never was a time when the scarecrow couldn't use another patch on his pants. Oh, by the way, step out where you can see that little bonnet with the green lilacs and the purple veil, Eddy. Isn't that something?"

"It would look better if it had a skirt under it. Maybe I can get you one from my Aunty Belle."

Mr. Hooke waved the idea away with both hands and a dibber. "Don't you do it," he roared. It was always difficult for Mr. Hooke to keep the storms of the St. Lawrence out of his voice; when he became excited he boomed and roared like a northwest gale. "Don't you do it, Eddy

Buckle," he shouted. "It's that little bonnet and the floating veil over those old dungarees that simply panics the crows. Why, this morning a couple winged over from One-Tree Island, took a look, put on the brakes, and sheered off for The Center, and not a sign of them coming back this way, either. Oliver Binns, too. Even that tough old cat is leery of the purple veil since he caught his claw in it. And that makes me think, you haven't seen anything of Oliver lately, have you, Eddy?"

"I've got him with me."

"I suspected as much."

"It was Oliver's turn to earn something for the Chests, after all the sardines I bought him. So I took him to the pet show and——"

"What pet show?"

"Well, it really wasn't a pet show, after all. You see, my notice was torn at the corner, right through the word petunia. It was a petunia show—gosh! An' Oliver smelling like——"

"I can imagine. Well, well, well, so Mr. Binns has been exhibited in a flower show. Wonders will never cease. That is," grinned Mr. Hooke, "as long as we have a Buckle in the neighborhood."

"Anyway, he got the prize."

"He got—who got—what's that again, Eddy?"

"Oliver got the five dollar prize. The trick now is to make Miss Binns understand that he should give it to the Chests. Piet came along to help me."

"I'll help you, son." Mr. Hooke tossed his dibber under the hedge and dusted his hands. "It'll take all of us talking together to make Miss Tissy believe that her cat has been honored as a 'Best Petunia,' and I wouldn't blame her; but I want to help."

There was a plate of chopped food on the Binns's back step and Miss Tissy stood beside it, rubbing catnip between her hands. The air was fragrant with it. She wasn't pleased to see Mr. Hooke turn in at her gate, along with two boys and a covered basket. But when she heard a fierce yeowl-l-l-l, she started down the path to meet them.

"I heard my cat just now," she quavered. "Is he—is he in that basket?"

"That he is, Miss," said Piet, pleasantly. "Hale and hearty, and honored by all. Took first prize at the show, he did."

"Yes, ma'am, Tissy, believe it or not, that old black bruiser won five dollars for being the best petunia in Cliffton Center," roared Mr. Hooke, quite loud enough for any listener in Braeside to have heard all. "Eddy Buckle took him there."

"Put the basket down, Piet," said Eddy solemnly. And then, nodding to the plate of chopped food on the step, he asked, "What's that?"

Miss Tissy replied that it was sardines. "Chopped sardines and catnip will bring Oliver home from anywhere," she said.

Eddy doubted it. "Not after he's had so many that they leak through," he sniffed. "Sardines are no treat to Oliver now, ma'am. Tell her about the money in his locket again, sir, before I open the basket."

Mr. Hooke went over the day's proceedings once more in detail. He enlarged upon the matter of the Chests of Cheer and the why and wherefore of Oliver's labors in its behalf. Miss Tissy brushed him aside.

"Oh, my beautiful, beautiful darling," she squeaked excitedly, meaning Oliver and not Mr. Hooke, of course. "Now I guess some of the Braeside folks will have to change their opinions, all right. That Captain Todd, chasing poor Oliver with a rake clear down to the dock just because he got inside the kitchen and ate ten perch that were all ready for the frying pan. Why doesn't Captain Todd keep his doors closed? And Mrs. Mold complaining that Oliver digs up her rose beds. And Mr. Liggard borrowing Oliver to kill a rat in his attic like he did that time when the rat chased Oliver down the back stairs and they both ran right up Mr. Liggard's leg. It served him right. Oliver doesn't have to like rats any better than the Liggards, does he? And Mr. Moom bawling him out for taking a nap now and then on his old green rooster's back. And you, Mr. Hooke, and your scarecrow. And Milly Witchit claiming that cats give her the asthma. Every last one of you finding fault with Oliver instead of appreciating him. Let me see his prize."

Eddy unbuttoned his blouse and removed a cartwheel

of shirred blue ribbon. "It was a mistake," he explained honestly. "Oliver isn't a flower, you know. But the judges said that if it had been a pet show instead of what it was, he probably would have won this thing just the same." He handed the fancy blue ornament to Miss Binns and she clasped it to her breast.

"Of course," she cried proudly. "Of course. I shall keep this forever and ever."

Eddy was afraid of that. Miss Tissy seemed to him to be the kind of a woman who would keep her hands forever and ever on all the prizes she could get hold of. He was grateful, now, for Mr. Hooke's support. Stepping close to his Braeside friend's side, he demanded boldly, "How about the five dollar prize?"

"The—where is this other prize?"

"In the cat's locket, Tissy," boomed Mr. Hooke. "The lads are honest enough to think the bill belongs to Oliver, but I say it's time that old black pest took a little interest, made a little sackerfize—you know the flat brown basket in the store—and did a little work for the poor people over where the war is, same as the rest of us. You've signed up, you know, with Eddy here to keep your walk cleaned."

"But of course Oliver would want to donate his five dollars to the Chests of Cheer," said Miss Binns at once. "What in the world are you bellowing about?"

"Open the basket, Piet," shrilled Eddy above the hub-bub.

Oliver boiled into view like a black stew out of a soup pot, but Piet was quicker still. He grasped the enraged animal by the collar, lifted him in his arms, and, scratching soothingly behind the black, furry ears, reminded Oliver again and again that he was a gorgeous, gorgeous puss. Mr. Binns relaxed and purred like a well-oiled motor.

And Miss Binns gasped. "Well," she said just as soon as she could speak at all. "For goodness sake. Oliver appears to like you, boy. I never saw him take to anyone before."

"He's a gorgeous puss, ma'am. I should enjoy a visit with him now and then, if it were permitted. I had a cat like this when we lived in Dover, taught him several amusing tricks, and he was no smarter than this chap, I assure you."

"I hope you will visit him, us, often. I trust Oliver's judgment in picking friends almost above my own," said Miss Tissy Binns primly. "What did you say your name was, boy?"

"Piet. I'm Eddy's partner."

"Oh, I see. But you said that you lived in Dover. Do you mean Dover, England?"

"Yes, ma'am. I wonder if you may have heard of my Aunty Penelope Paxton who once lived in Cliffton Center."

"No. I never did, Piet."

"Oh, sorry. Well, shall we go, for now, Eddy? We have work to do, you know."

On his way back to the gate, Piet glanced to this side and that across the hedges and gardens of Braeside. "Snug," he said wistfully. "Quite like home, it is. The same smell of damp loam and wallflowers, and thyme that has been trodden on flagstone paths. And blue water beyond. And kind people. Miss Binns is a very, very nice lady."

"You wouldn't have thought so last week if you had been with us when Mr. Watson pulled us down the road," Eddy sniffed. "He had to leave us in the swale because she hollered so at us. She said she wouldn't have our house in Braeside, that Mr. Watson couldn't do that to 'em. Golly! I don't mind telling you, Piet, that I never expected to see this five dollar bill again. Hey-y-y, where's Ol' Love? There's nothing in Nero any more, Piet."

"Yoo-hoo-oo-o, Piet. Here I am."

Piet lifted shocked eyes to a pile of hedge clippings in the distance, caught a glimmer of pink, and swooped upon it like a barn swallow on a moth. "Ol' Love," he cried. "What happened, lass?"

"S-sssh!" Rosalove peeped, wide-eyed, out of the greenery. "I think somebody is listening behind the hedge."

"But why are you in the street when you should have——"

"I couldn't hide in the cart any longer, Piet, not after I stood up to see where you and Eddy had gone and saw this! Tell Eddy to hurry; I want to ask him something."

"He's got to wake the horse first, Ol' Love; that will take time. What was it you saw?"

"Back away into the street and then look up on top of the hedge right over my head."

Piet did as requested. "Gar," he choked. "A yew cock!"

"Just like the one in Freel's garden, Piet."

"Only better. Bigger and more active like."

"The Freel's had a peacock on the other side of their gate."

"But the cock was the best. Only not half as good as this."

"It's a bit of home, isn't it, Piet? I hid here and said to myself, 'Mom'll be coming out the gate any minute now, just you wait and see.' Only she didn't, of course. But it was a rare comfort pretending."

"Harr-rr-rrumph!"

"Down, lass," warned Piet, leaping forward to stand between the quiet pile of hedge clippings and the gate. "Somebody's coming."

And at just that moment, Mark clattered up to the forbidden lower end of Braeside and Eddy, jumping from the driver's plank in Nero, shivered to find himself face to face with Mr. Moom. Mr. Moom drew his shaggy brows into a terrific frown. "All over the place already, eh?" he said bitterly. "You who promised to stay away from me with that horse and cart until invited."

"I lost a little girl, sir," Eddy apologized bravely. "Just as soon as we find her——"

"You don't think I have her, do you? Are you—harr-rr-rrumph—are you the one who commented upon my cock just now?" he asked, wheeling most unexpectedly to face Piet.

"Yes, sir. You have a very, very good cock."

"I have, eh?"

"Oh quite. As true a bit of clipping as could be found anywhere. There's a curve to the neck that even the Freels couldn't get."

"What Freels?"

"The Freels of Dover, sir. Very fine farm near the cliffs."

"Piet was there when he was bombed out."

"My ears are good, Eddy, and Mr. Hooke can be heard a mile away in foggy weather. I didn't miss any of the story that was poured out across the way, in Miss Tissy's garden. There was no small girl in your company then, however."

"No, sir. That's what I tried to tell you. She was hiding in Nero because she wasn't invited into Braeside, but she worried over Piet when we stayed so long with Mr. Hooke and Miss Binns, and she stood up to look for us, and she saw your cock."

"And I know the rest. Except—harr-rr-rrumph—where she is now."

A tiny hand reached up out of the pile of greenstuffs almost at his very feet and took a firm hold on Mr. Moom's surprised old fingers. He looked downward. And then he pulled Rosalove forth to the full sunlight. Another sharp look, and he had Rosalove riding high on his crooked elbow. "Well, God bless my soul!" he said.

Rosalove laid her soft little cheek against Mr. Moom's scrubby wrinkles and chuckled. "He's just like Gaffer Sam, Piet," she whispered. "You don't need to fear him."

"Gar," gasped Piet.

"And who," demanded Mr. Moom with another terrible frown, "is Gaffer Sam?"

Rosalove chuckled again, but she turned all explanations over to Piet. And while she waited, she kissed Mr. Moom gently on the chin. So it is not to be wondered at that he missed most of Piet's words until the part about the pig was reached. Then Mr. Moom looked up.

"Pig?" he asked. "What pig?"

"Gaffer Sam's, sir. Or rather, they belonged to the Freels and Gaffer Sam tended them. He was as cantankerous an old nizy as could be found in a dozen shires. He would shake his staff and mouth crazy words at anybody who drew near the oak tree where he hunkered all day long, minding the fat white pigs that rooted about. But Ol' Love had a fondness for him, and he for her. She'd take his staff away to play with, and he cut her many sets of doll dishes from the fallen acorns. Gaffer Sam and Ol' Love were on very cordial terms."

"He means that Ol' Love liked the old crosspatch," Eddy explained hastily. "Piet talks funny, sometimes."

"I understood all I wanted to, lad." Mr. Moom frowned

and shook his shaggy head. "Pigs, indeed. So I'm like a crazy old pig tender, am I? That, my small maid with the pink bow in her hair, is something that needs to be sweetened with another kiss before it can be swallowed."

Rosalove sweetened it gladly. And then Mr. Moom invited them, all three, inside the gate so that Mrs. Moom could watch Rosalove do it again.

Mrs. Moom was not at all like Mr. Moom. She was delicate and slender, silvery white from the topmost curl of her pretty head to the shining clasp of her tiny slipper. She was sitting on the side porch in a low chair that was like a basket of roses, looking at the river. Eddy had never seen his mother sitting like that with her hands quietly clasped in her white lap; he thought that Mrs. Moom must be ill and so he approached the side porch on tiptoes. He was surprised by Mrs. Moom's bright brown eyes, her rosy cheeks, and her gay smile when she turned her head as the screen door to the side porch opened.

"Well, upon my word, boys!" said Mrs. Moom. "And one sweet girl. You do bring home the nicest things, dear. Won't you find stools for all our callers? I was just watching the gulls over Jackstraw Lighthouse."

Piet shoved a cushioned stool across the floor and sat close to Mrs. Moom, nodding his head toward the gulls. "Like the terns above our Dover cliffs," he said. "They might be cousins."

"And who knows that they aren't?" asked Mrs. Moom. "That beautiful chap swooping about out there looking for fish in the shallows may have ridden a storm cloud during some wild night from Dover to us, and that great billow just making ready to crash against our sea wall may have started its journey as a tiny ripple along the English coast. It's fun to sit and watch the river, anyway, and make up stories about it."

"Piet and Ol' Love started from the English coast, and they rode through storm clouds on some wild nights, and they washed up on our shores," said Eddy, looking at the white-capped billows with a shudder. "Golly! I'm glad I'm not a gull, or a wave in the river, or a war kid. I've got plenty of wild riding in Nero, now that Mark's beginning to get his strength back. But it's over ruts an' through dust, not on top of all that slithery water. I don't like too much water."

"Not even to sit and watch it? It's never two minutes the same. Sometimes it sparkles and dances and laughs, and then it seems old and tired and heavy as a river of lead."

"I've got too much to do besides sitting and watching a river."

Mrs. Moom turned her head and appeared to notice Eddy for the first time. "You are the businessman among the Buckles, aren't you?" she asked pleasantly. "The money maker?"

"We all earn money for the Chests. I guess I'll have more than the rest, as soon as I get around to it, even with giving half of what I make to Piet."

"Why should you do that, Eddy?"

"For his mom." Eddy explained the arrangement proudly. He took the occasion to lay the problem of a Braeside seamstress before the Mooms, saying that he wanted to get as much done for the strangers as he could before Mr. Watson appeared to move the little tenant house down the road. "If I could help get Piet's mom started," he concluded, "an' find his Aunty Penelope, why then I could spend all my time on my collectin' job. You don't know any Aunty Penelope Paxton around here, do you?"

"I don't, dear. How much are you expecting to take in with your collecting job, Eddy?"

"Fifty cents for each lot front, three dollars and fifty cents a week."

"But there are eight lots in Braeside, Eddy. Why not four dollars each week?"

Eddy turned his back on Mr. Moom and watched the gulls over Jackstraw Lighthouse with forced interest. "Golly, don't they squall," he said.

"They do, indeed. But about that four dollars, Eddy. It seems to me there must be somebody in Braeside who is refusing to become a regular customer of yours. I wonder who it could be."

"Squalling, squalling all the time," said Eddy, his glassy eyes fixed above Jackstraw Lighthouse.

"Do you know why anybody in Braeside would be unwilling to help you in your fine work, Eddy?"

"Maybe they think a fat man on my chariot don't look so good in a street like this. I could paint him out, though, when I get around to it."

"Don't you do it," cried Mr. and Mrs. Moom in the same breath.

Eddy began to feel dizzy. He fixed his attention on the gulls, one, two, three. A fourth disappeared behind a puffy cloud before he could count it and Mr. Moom guffawed hoarsely.

"Three will do nicely, Eddy," he said as soon as he could speak at all. "We don't need that fourth chap. I'm the culprit, my dear," he added, patting Mrs. Moom's arm gently. "As you have guessed. But how was I to know the Buckles were what they are? How was I to know that that horse and chariot would be good for a fit of laughing every time they rumbled along the street? And haven't we needed a bit of fun in Braeside this long, long time? But how, above all else, was I to know that the Buckles scattered seeds of friendliness right and left and part of the harvest from such sowing would be a little lass with a pink bow in her brown curls?" He drew Ol' Love closer to him and she patted his arm gently, as he had patted Mrs. Moom's.

Mrs. Moom had no answers for all these questions. All she said was that she knew where the Mooms kept their seeds of friendliness if he didn't. But Mr. Moom did. "I was coming to that, my dear," he told her pleasantly. And then, turning to Eddy, he added, "Count me in as one of

your regular customers, son. With double pay on the days
I trim the cock."

For a moment, Eddy was stunned. But only for a moment. "Golly, Piet," he gasped, "he trimmed it today. I
saw him getting the ladder out before I went to the pet
—er—the flower show. Lucky we brought the rake an'
broom along; we could start right in at the bottom of the
street, now, and work along toward the swale."

Mrs. Moom interrupted by asking Piet to tinkle the
little silver bell on the table at his elbow, and when he
did so, Prissy, the Moom's housekeeper, appeared like a
Jack-in-the-box with a tray of seed cookies and a tall, misted
pitcher of ice-cold lemonade.

Eddy made no objections to a glass of lemonade. Nor
to a second. He accepted a third silently. Prissy returned
to fill the tall pitcher again and again. It began to look
as if the race between Eddy and the lemonade pitcher
might be a close one. It ended abruptly, however, when
Mr. Moom asked Mrs. Moom how she would like to have
a little maid with a pink bow in her curls around the place
all the time and Mrs. Moom replied that the only thing
she could think of that would be better would be to have
a little maid and a brother by the name of Piet. Eddy's
glass smacked the tray and the party was over. He was
grieved and he didn't care who knew it. Once again he
had found treachery where he had expected nothing but
fair play.

"Just like Bandlo!" he said, looking at the Mooms

reproachfully. "Pretending to be so nice just to fool me. But when I got home, Bandlo's cart had no back to it; and after I've drunk up all your lemonade, you try to get my war kids away from me. These are my war kids, I'd have you know. I got 'em out of a petunia show. If you want some, why don't you go to Gananoque like Mr. Watson did an' get 'em from a committee?" Every golden hair on Eddy's head stood on end in bitter protest. "Don't try to wheedle mine away from me. Pull Ol' Love off his knee, Piet, an' come on outside."

Mrs. Moom sat upright in the chair that was like a basket of roses and held out both slender white hands entreatingly. "Wait, Eddy," she begged. "We wouldn't hurt you for the world. We were just happy and thoughtless. Or rather, we were both thinking of this great empty house and your little crowded——"

"Our house isn't so little." Eddy saw nothing to clap hands about in her apology, as yet. "An' it isn't crowded. There's lots of room in it."

"But my dear, so many Buckles."

"There's never too many Buckles."

"Right," said Mr. Moom briskly, rising to his feet and putting Ol' Love gently on hers. He swept all that remained of the platter of seed cookies onto a sheet of the morning paper, twisted the corners together, and handed the packet to Eddy. "For Mark, with my best wishes," he added formally. "May we meet again some day on the County Road under happier circumstances. And you might whisper into his ear," he concluded, opening the screen door for his departing guests, "that I consider him very fortunate to be a Buckle. Very fortunate, indeed."

Eddy knew a real apology when he heard it and he accepted it like a gentleman. "That's more like it," he said stiffly. "Thanks for Mark's treat. And thanks for becoming a regular customer. Terms are fifty cents a week, on Sat'-day, at about five o'clock, strictly cash. We won't trample your garden or hurt your cock."

"But you will call again and often, won't you?" begged Mrs. Moom. Eddy made no reply.

11. Eddy Makes a Mistake

THE bright sun of another morning was shining down upon the little tenant house beside the swale. Mrs. Buckle was beating egg whites into stiff, snowy peaks and Fan was watching her. Fan was not helping herself to sugar lumps or raisins from the opened boxes roundabout and that was singular enough to stir her mother's curiosity.

"Anything wrong outside, deary?" asked Mrs. Buckle.

Fan shook her head. "Do you know how long we've been here waiting for Mr. Watson, Mother?" she sighed.

"I should, lovey. Just one week ago today. Well, well, well! We'll have to give ourselves a birthday supper tonight and put one candle on the cake to celebrate."

A quick smile lifted the corners of Fan's mouth, but it was gone again before it had brightened the gloom around the table to any great extent. "I could wish on a lily for him to hurry up an' come back," she said soberly, much too soberly for her. "But I don't dare to. I'm too magic, Mother."

Mrs. Buckle stopped beating egg whites and stared at the mite in the pink sunsuit. "Magic?" she repeated. "I never noticed it."

"But I am. I wouldn't even dare to wish on a—on an onion even. No, sir, not even on an onion."

"Oh fudge." Mrs. Buckle began clattering her egg beater against the yellow mixing bowl. "George told me all about that lily game," she chuckled. "I don't see that you've got anything to worry about there."

"Did he tell you what the first wish was?" she asked.

"Something about earning more money for the Chests, wasn't it, deary?"

"Yes. An' look what happened. Julia began to lay eggs, an' little Horace gets a dollar for nothing from Mr. Liggard, an' Mrs. Witchit can't put enough on the basket for Charles, an' what Eddy is going to make just as soon as he gets around to it is something terrible."

"I've been worrying a bit along that line too, sweety. It looks as if the Buckles would better move away from Braeside pretty quick or they'll be leaving the folks here poverty poor."

"But that's just it, Mother," Fan interrupted hastily. "I don't believe we ever will move away from here."

"You don't?"

"No, ma'am. 'Cause my second wish was that we wouldn't. An' what do you know, Captain Todd wished on a lily that very night, he just told me in secret, an' he wished that very same thing. Oh, we're stuck here, all right."

"Until Mr. Watson comes home." Mrs. Buckle laughed

merrily. "Then you'll see that a lily is nothing but a lily, and all this talk about magic is simply foolishness."

"Did George tell you what my third wish was?"

"If he did, I wasn't paying attention, lovey."

"I wished that we'd get some more alphabet."

"You aren't fretting about that one, I hope, sweety."

"Well, I was just over to Captain Todd's an' he asked me how the alphabet was growing an' I said we had to let O in after N-is-Nero. An' he wanted to know who O was, an' boy-y was I ashamed to tell him that we had to count O-is-Oliver 'cause that old black cat earned five dollars for the Chests. But I said that was all. We didn't have any P. An' he said how about Piet? P-is-Piet. What do you know!"

Mrs. Buckle was far from being disturbed. She scattered some white sugar on the egg whites and said, "I suppose he didn't mention that the next letter after P is Q, did he? If Q doesn't put an end to this alphabet non- sense——"

"But it won't, Mother." Fan began to buzz excitedly. "He said that Q was a crazy letter that never did anybody any good an' it belonged down among the X's, Y's, and Z's. He said for me to do like he did, shove it right down there an' forget all about it. He said Q, X, Y, and Z were barriers to keep the rest of the alphabet from running all over the place. So I took it away an' right off there was R. An' R-is-Rosalove. Now I guess you see how magic I am."

"Hand me the butter dish, deary. I suppose you didn't talk over S with the old captain, did you?

"Yes, I did. S-is-Skipper. Boy-y-y!"

Mrs. Buckle had nothing to say to that, but Fan had. "Eddy thinks I'm magic," she continued solemnly.

"Fol-de-rol! Where is Eddy, deary?"

"Down back in the elderberries, fixing Mark's harness. They all are down there, except Delia. She's over in the store with Julia's last egg. Eddy said for me to slap Q right after S-is-Skipper an' make it stick there. He said we didn't need any more alphabet in our family, an' for me to watch out how I wished on lilies after this. Golly, don't think I won't."

Rat-a-ta-tattttttt!

Mrs. Buckle broke another egg without meaning to. "What in the world was that?" she asked.

Fan flicked across the room and lifted the kitchen shade an inch. "It's Mr. Moom," she whispered. "Pounding us with his cane. But now he's crossed to the other side of the road again. The nerve of him, coming over to our side when he wasn't invited. Listen to him roar."

"At what, deary?"

"At Eddy, I guess. He says he wants Eddy Buckle. Hey-y, there comes Delia out of the store and Mr. Moom has stopped her."

Mrs. Buckle left her mixing table and, crossing to the window, opened it so that she could hear as well as see what was going on in front of the store.

"You're one of those Buckles to judge by your head," said Mr. Moom in his best Gaffer Sam manner. "Why doesn't Eddy come when he's called? I pounded on the house, too. Where is he?"

"He's in the swale, sir, getting Mark ready to begin collecting." Delia edged away from the store steps, but a second fat man puffing up Braeside from the dock blocked her flight across the County Road.

"No use trying any longer, the engine's dead," he barked at Mr. Moom. "Who's this girl, where's the boy?"

"This is Eddy's sister, I haven't been able to get hold of Eddy yet."

"Well, why not? We haven't got all the time in the world, you know, Moom. Ten o'clock will be here before you know it and what the committee will think when they learn that we were hanging around Braeside at ten o'clock instead of being in Cliffton Center, I can't imagine."

"I can," Mr. Moom replied hotly. "Particularly after I explain to them that we missed the meeting because of your stupidity in coming for me by water in a boat that fairly dropped apart the minute it touched the Braeside dock."

"Don't forget to add," the fat man pointed out bitterly, "that you called me on the phone to come and get you because your gas tank was empty. A car and a couple of station wagons on the place and not a drop of gas. There's brainwork for you. Would Captain Todd take us around to the city dock in THE MOLLY?"

"Not a chance when the river is as rough as it is today. What's your name, girl?"

"Delia, sir."

"Well, Delia, see how quick you can bring Eddy over here; tell him it's important."

Delia crossed the road like a butterfly. A second later her bright head peered around the front of Mr. Watson's trailer. "Eddy said, 'pinhooks!' " she piped.

"He said what?"

"Pinhooks, sir."

"What does pinhooks mean, Gorse?" asked Mr. Moom.

The two fat men turned to the trailer for more information, but the bright head had vanished. Delia had sharp ears and she had not missed a single word of Mr. Moom's question. Gorse. She flitted through the swale hissing warnings right and left, before scrambling from the orange box to the trailer and from the trailer to the kitchen of the little tenant house to take refuge, with Fan, behind the folds of their mother's apron.

She was none too soon. A nervous cane thumped against the trailer, a strange head blossomed above the doorsill. Once before a shaggy head had appeared there, calling for Eddy, but that call had been accompanied by a hail of peppermint balls. It was quite another thing to see a visitor, almost at your feet, bringing Mr. Gorse. The feminine Buckles pushed Mr. Moom as far away as they could with their cold stares. Before they could say anything, however, a curt voice from the swale took over.

"Come down out of there," said Eddy harshly. "What do you want of me? I'm busy."

"Well, God bless my—harr-rr-umph!" said Mr. Moom, dropping away from the orange box. "I didn't see you before, Eddy."

He might have added that he hadn't seen Charles, George, or little Horace before either, but he saw them now. They stood at Eddy's elbow, watchfully waiting.

"Hello, hello, hello, one and all." Mr. Moom spread his greeting around the quartet. "Where's Ol' Love this bright morning?"

Charles, George, and little Horace closed in, but Eddy moved them backward with a glance. "What do you want?" he repeated, steel in his voice. "I've got my collectin' to do."

"Well, I wouldn't think there was much of a rush about that, son. You could do it later, couldn't you?"

"I'm always doing it later. I never get started."

"But why the grouch, Eddy? I thought we parted good friends last night."

"Come, come, Moom, you're wasting valuable time," the second fat man interrupted. "Get to the point."

At the sound of his voice the Buckles quivered like race horses waiting for the starting signal. But let us say this much for them, they did wait, when they could so easily have upset this man into the swale and laid the blame on slippery elderberry and dogwood roots that twisted every which way through the mire.

"The point," said Mr. Moom, "is that Mr. Gorse and I have most important business in The Center at ten o'clock, and no way to keep our appointment unless you will help us out. You, Eddy, have the only gasless, engineless conveyance in Braeside at the present moment, believe it or not. How about it?"

"Do you mean Mark?"

"And, by golly, the Roman chariot."

"Get in," said Eddy, pointing to Nero. "You'll have to climb the slats. An' the fare will be one dollar."

"One dollar!" Mr. Gorse appeared to be on the point of kicking the slats instead of climbing them, but Eddy changed his mind for him.

"Step light when you get in," he warned. "Nero's back'll keep trash from spilling out all right, but I never figured on loading two fat men inside there. A busted slat would cost you heavy, you know."

"One dollar for a neighborly lift to The Center in a silly play cart like this," bellowed Mr. Gorse. "Where do we sit?"

Nobody answered because Eddy had disappeared into the swale on the pretext of cutting an elderberry switch for Mark's use. "Psst-t-t, Eddy," whispered Piet, on his face among the silky dogwood roots. "That's *the* Mr. Gorse."

"You're telling me." Eddy made a great thrashing among the elderberries. "I heard them over by the store. An' I heard Delia, too."

"Would he be looking for Ol' Love and me, do you think?"

"Who else? Says he wants to get to the committee as fast as he can. Well, he will all right, all right. He'll get away from here, anyway. That's the only reason I'm taking him down the road in Nero. You an' Ol' Love keep under cover till I get back, an' if Mr. Watson comes first tell him where I went an' to wait for me. I won't be long."

Eddy climbed to the driver's plank above Nero's pink nightgown and said, "Gaddup-p-p!" A touch of the elderberry switch helped to waken Mark.

"Are we going to stand all the way to The Center?" roared Mr. Gorse.

"If you can," Eddy told him calmly. " 'Cause I'll be going fast, once Mark wakes up. Get a handful of him somewhere in front, Charles, an' pull. George an' Horace, you get behind Nero an' push. Now then, everybody yell all together."

"Gaddup-p-p-p-p!" shouted four Buckles with all their might.

Mark left the swale like a Flying Tiger. He traveled the County Road in a puff of dust with the river breeze behind it. And just when it began to look as if he might sprout wings and take off for the stars and points beyond Eddy shouted, "Whoa-a-a-a!"

Mark whoa-ed on two feet. And Mr. Gorse cracked into Mr. Moom like a glass of jelly that was being very carelessly handled. "Oh, oh, oh!" he groaned, although Mr. Moom, it would seem, had the greater cause for complaint. "My knee, oh, oh, oh! Those are my spectacles on your vest button, Moom! Oh, oh, oh!"

"Take it a bit easier, Eddy," begged Mr. Moom. "It'll be all right if we don't meet that committee until ten thirty."

Eddy twisted about on his plank and gazed down into Nero chidingly. "Is that the committee about war kids?" he asked.

"Why yes, you might call it that."

"Then you could get out and walk the rest of the way."

"We could get out and——"

Mr. Moom prevented Mr. Gorse from finishing what was in his mind. "Careful, Gorse," he warned. "You might start this horse to sneezing. You don't know about that, but I do."

"But that little—that little——"

"I know he's little. He knows he's little. All the Buckles are little. It doesn't keep them from being smart."

"We paid him a dollar to get us to the bank."

"We haven't paid him a cent as yet," replied Mr. Moom.

"An' I wouldn't take a cent," Eddy made haste to assure everybody. "Don't think it. Shady Rest Cabins, Hamburgers, Antiques are just ahead of you over there and you could hire Mr. Wente to take you the rest of the way in his car. I want to earn all the money I can for

the Chests, sure I do. But there are some things I just can't stomach."

"Does he—he can't mean us, does he, Moom?" asked Mr. Gorse.

"He certainly can, and does," Mr. Moom replied, with an unexpected guffaw. "Over the slats with you."

"Aren't you coming with me?"

"Later. Tell Wente to wait out in the road for me."

As soon as they were alone Mr. Moom shoved his hat to the back of his head and said, "Now then, Eddy, what's the idea?"

"You know all right, all right."

"I'm as innocent as a snow-white petunia bell. And nobody, I should think, could fool you twice on the subject of petunias."

Eddy blushed. His head, however, remained unbowed. "I could be fooled on lots of things, I guess. Once, anyway," he confessed bitterly. "But I do know what a flower show is now and I wouldn't ever take another cat there; and I do know what you mean when you invite me into your place an' fill me up on lemonade. I wouldn't ever take another war kid there."

"You aren't by any chance speaking of Piet and Ol' Love, are you, Eddy?" asked Mr. Moom.

"Sure I am. Mr. Watson'll be back today probably an' he'll see that you don't turn 'em over to that old committee."

Mr. Moom had never been so bewildered in all his life.

He felt that he was going to lose his patience in a minute and roar, and he didn't want to do that until he found what this business was all about. He tried to keep his voice down to a gentle boom, at least. What committee shouldn't I turn them over to? And why not? Now then, answer those questions, my lad."

Eddy could, and did. Stingingly. "That old Gorse's committee!" His glance flicked up the road to the nervous figure that was nearing Shady Rest Cabins, Hamburgers, Antiques. "He'll never get my war kids again, even if you did bring him out here so he could find them. We know places in our swale, now, where Piet an' Ol' Love can lie flat in the mud like they did this morning an' you could never, never, never find them."

"Ol' Love in the mud? Well, God bless my soul."

"She'd rather be there," Eddy continued, "than back with Mrs. Gorse an' her liver. No fried fish an' potatoes, either. An' the worst looking old green plaid dress. Sobbing onto Skipper all the time, too. Why, Ol' Love doesn't know where Skipper is half the time since she has been at our house. Fan has to keep track of him for her. That's how much sobbing she does with us. An' you tried to turn her back over to the committee. Golly."

"You believe that, do you, Eddy?" said Mr. Moom sadly.

"Well, you brought old Gorse out here to our house. How would he have known about Piet an' Ol' Love except you told him?"

"I'll tell you how, my boy. Your mother phoned from the store to Mrs. Gorse right after they arrived. Gorse was telling me about it just as soon as he came up from the dock this morning. He wanted me to keep the children out of his sight for fear they would want to go back to The Center with him. He and Mrs. Gorse are too busy just now to bother with children. Get this, Eddy—they don't want Piet or Ol' Love."

"But, but you said you were going to the committee."

"There are probably as many committees in the Center as there are ants in the Braeside peony beds." Mr. Moom pursed his lips and considered the matter of committees. "As many, if not more," was his final conclusion. "And all different. I don't suppose there is a person on the committee that is now meeting at the bank, with the possible exception of a man named Moom, who would have the slightest interest in what you call 'war kids.'"

It was Eddy's turn to feel dizzy. Of course, he remembered now, his mother had crossed the road to the store and phoned to the Gorses just as soon as Piet and Ol' Love had finished their first dinner in the little tenant house. "Golly, maybe I made a mistake," he told himself. Still, there was something here that needed more explaining. He felt it without knowing exactly what it was. He turned around on the driver's plank and looked along the County Road toward The Center.

"Hey-y," he warned sharply, "Mr. Wente's backing out of Shady Rest Cabins, Hamburgers, Antiques in his car."

"Let him."

"But Mr. Gorse is waving for you to hurry up."

"Let him, too. It's only ten minutes past ten. Plenty of time to reach the bank by ten thirty."

"Not the way Mr. Wente has to drive that old car of his nowadays. His engine isn't any too good an' he won't be surprised to hear that back tire blow any minute."

"That's his worry." Mr. Moom leaned comfortably back against Nero's slats and grinned. "This is one trip to The Center when I'm not fretting about engines, gas, or tires," he added. "Now, to return to more important affairs. Mr. Gorse came to Braeside this morning after me, my lad, believe it or not. Because he had just received great news and had whipped up a committee to handle it and he wanted me and my check book on it and I told him over the phone that if he wanted me he'd have to come and get me. The old zany came in a boat. You couldn't guess what's going on at The Center tomorrow, could you?"

Eddy shook his head.

"Of course you couldn't, unless you heard about it at the store," Mr. Moom continued. "Well, a Princess is going to pass through town on her way to Canada."

"A real Princess?"

"Real enough, though Dutch. She's going to have her two babies and quite a crowd of folks with her, and the Gorses think it will be a treat for us all to gaze upon royalty. They're going to see that the whole place is

draped in bunting, pennants, evergreens, and red, white, and blue streamers. Mr. Gorse is going to have tomorrow declared a holiday hereabouts."

Eddy was crushed. "Golly, I should say I did make a mistake," he muttered. And then, quite loud enough for Mr. Moom to hear, he added, "The mistakes I do make, sir. Pet shows an' everything. But this beats them all. I'm sorry what I said about you an' your lemonade, Mr. Moom. I'll hustle right back to Braeside an' I'll have your place so cleaned up you won't know it by the time you come home."

"That would be nice, very nice indeed," Mr. Moom replied, not quite as cordially as Eddy would have liked, however. "But I don't mind telling you, son, that my feelings have been hurt. When I think of Ol' Love hiding from me with her little face in the mire——"

Eddy brightened. He knew now how to bring comfort and make amends at the same time. "Don't fret over her," he said confidently. "Fan will have her out of the swale an' all scrubbed up with pink soap by this time. In a clean pink sunsuit, too. With another bow in her hair. An' I tell you what I'll do. I'll bring her down the street this afternoon to watch you clip the cock an' tell you some more about Gaffer Sam. Would you like that, sir?"

"If you do that, Eddy, all between us will be forgiven and forgotten," Mr. Moom promised.

"I'll do better than that," said Eddy, who could be generous as well as just. "I'll bring Piet, too. He likes to look at Mrs. Moom. He says she reminds him of Freel's clock."

"Freel's what?"

"His clock, sir. It was planted on the green in front of the Freel's byre, and it was just one solid mass of white baby roses. Round, of course, like a clock's face. The numbers were made by little bushes of red roses. In the middle there was a silver staff with a snowy dove perched atop. The sun fell on the dove, you see, an' cast a long shadow that traveled about the clock's face all day long. Piet's mom said that hours are sweeter when you read them in red and white roses. It's Mrs. Moom's being so white with chairs and cushions covered with roses all around her that made Piet say she reminded him of Freel's clock, sir."

"She'll like to hear that, Eddy."

"Piet's mom loved the baby roses more than anything else at Freel's. She was on her way to clip them when a bomb fell right smack on top of the white dove."

"God help us all."

"Yes, sir, He did. Nobody at Freel's was killed but——
Hey-y, Mr. Gorse has gone on to the committee without
you."

Mr. Moom had another look at his watch. "Ten twenty-
five," he said. "Well, too bad. I'm afraid they'll have to
plan a holiday without me this time."

"Pinhooks!" Eddy flipped about on his plank and gathered the reins in his hands. "Mark could beat that old
car of Mr. Wente's with both eyes shut," he boasted. "But
when he's got 'em wide open like now an' all his strength
back, you've got nothing to worry about. Only, maybe,
how to keep from bouncing out of Nero. Of course I
didn't figure on you when I nailed the slats on. Do you
think you can hang onto the sides, sir?"

"If I go out of Nero the fat man in the pink nightgown
goes with me. But how about you, Eddy?" Mr. Moom
asked as an afterthought. "What's to prevent you from
being tossed off that plank?"

"You, sir. Today." Eddy lifted his elderberry switch.
"That's another mistake I made," he confessed. "I didn't
know how fast Mark could travel an' so I put the driver's
seat on top of the king instead of in back there. I'm going
to change it just as soon as I get around to it, but I don't
seem to have much spare time. I guess you'll have to
reach over with one hand an' hang onto my pants in back
somewheres. Could you do that, sir?"

"I've got you, lad." Mr. Moom did better than requested. He reached out one long arm and held Eddy

firmly against his vest. "Where you go, I go and Nero goes, and I don't think Mark would want to lose all his friends at once. I've got a better opinion of him than that. All I hope is that the full committee is assembled in front of the bank when we arrive, and that we arrive ahead of Gorse."

Eddy swept Mark's ridges with the elderberry switch. "We will! Gaddup, Mark," he said. "Gaddup-p-p-p-p!"

12. The Little Tenant House Gives up Traveling

THE little tenant house was positively zippy with excitement. Breakfast with the Buckles was never exactly a dull affair, but if there was anything that could spice it nicely it was a Holiday. And here was a second one in the same week.

"Two. Two Holidays in one week," squealed Fan, tucking a bit of bread under a thick slab of butter. "That is if you could call the other thing a Holiday. We didn't even get to The Center on account of Mark running away an' Eddy chasing him with only his shirt on."

"It was pretty good on the slanting pasture, though," George reminded her. She agreed with him promptly.

"It was grand," she said. "An alphabet should always stay on a hillside so the army won't—— Mother, what are you doing?"

"Getting out the basins and tubs, deary. You could help Delia set up the screen if you have finished eating."

"But baths—not baths, Moth-er-r!"

"Baths it is. A hot scrub for everybody."

"For goodness sake, can't anybody ever get up an' just walk off to a Holiday the way he is?"

"Not you, lovey. The way your hair looks this minute——"

Fan's wail shook the stove lids. "Nobody's going to wash my hair, or brush it, either," she anounced. "Next thing I'll have to be wearing those tight buckled slippers."

"Lay them out for her, Delia deary."

"Not my old sneaks? Boy-y-y! What's the good of a Holiday?"

"Oh come now, you want to honor the little Princesses I should hope, lovey. Lay out a fresh pink sunsuit for Ol' Love too, Delia."

"Will the little Princesses wear their best crowns, Mother?" Fan licked the butter off her fingers slowly. "The ones with the di'monds in 'em?"

"They'd better," George growled. "With old Gorse watching them."

Fan turned her attention upon her twin. "Are you going to wear a necktie, George?" she asked.

"No!" George was shocked at the thought.

"I bet you are, just the same. Isn't George going to wear a necktie, Mother?"

"He sure is, sweety. And the less grumbling I hear from now on about baths, tight shoes, or neckties the better it will be for all concerned."

The Buckles recognized a blind alley when they found themselves in it as well as the next one. Knew what to do about it, too. They backed out in a hurry. After all, they had plenty of subjects for conversation besides this. There was always Aunty Belle, for instance.

"I wish we didn't have to go to Aunty Belle's for lunch," said Charles. "It would be lots more fun to take the covered basket and——"

"Rozb'ry san'wiches, ham san'wiches, an' b'nanas," piped little Horace. "Why can't we take the basket, Mother, an' eat our lunch on the main dock?"

"And I don't want to hear any more grumbling about Aunty Belle," said Mrs. Buckle firmly. "We won't bring up the subject of what to do with the Vics, either, if you please."

This order rather hampered the alphabet. "Law me," sighed Fan, wiping her fingers on her knees and pushing back from the table. "Nothing to talk about an' nothing to do but scrub. I'm going across the road for a minute, Mother."

"If you aren't back by the time the kettle boils——"

"I will be."

She was. Indeed, she was. The kettle was no more than beginning to make up its mind to steam at the spout when Fan came flying back to the little tenant house with an entirely new outlook on the day's festivities.

"Everybody's bathing," she cried, scrambling over the doorsill. "You never saw anything like it. Captain Todd just came in from a swim off the dock an' he's putting on his best blue suit, the one with the brass buttons all over it, an' you ought to see his necktie, George Buckle. Tight enough to make his tongue hang out, he said. Where's my pink rose soap?" She buzzed among her treasures in the corner behind the screen. "Somebody come in here an' scrub my hair," she demanded loudly. "I've got to have it brushed and fluffed out an' a pink bow in it, like Ol' Love's. Captain Todd likes it that way. Hurry up, everybody, we've got to be finished an' out front in just an hour."

"Why have we?" asked Charles, Delia, Eddy, George, and little Horace in one outcry.

"Because all the Braeside folks are going to meet on the store steps in an hour an' Mr. Moom is going to take them all in to the Holiday in his station wagons an' his biggest car. Mr. Moom is going to drive one of the station wagons, an' Mr. Liggard the other, an' Prissy's going to drive the car with Mrs. Moom in it. An' Captain Todd said that Mrs. Moom sent word by him to have Piet an' some of us go with her, an' Mr. Moom wants Ol' Love an' Eddy an' George an' me in the station wagon with him, an' the rest can go in the other station wagon with Mr. Liggard, an'——"

"Fan!" The little tenant house caught its breath and was still. Fan snapped her sentence in the middle, allowing the last words to drop where they would. When nothing but the clock on the shelf could be heard ticking merrily along, Mrs. Buckle asked quietly, "Now then, Fan sweety, just what did you tell Captain Todd?"

"I told him no."

"Well, that's better. You thanked him though, I hope."

"Yes'm. I told him we were going to the Holiday in our own cart an' he roared an' said we'd bust the slats off the back. And I said no we wouldn't, 'cause Eddy had fitted us into it an' we all went fine, only not the covered basket. But—but I did tell him——"

"Yes, deary?"

"I did tell him that we'd be glad to meet with the folks out in front of the store in an hour, an' start just when they all did, an' if they'd kind of take it easy so as not to tire Mark out, we'd help 'em make a nice long p'rade into The Center."

Nobody ever saw anything lovelier than all those Buckles when, an hour later, they fluttered around the corner of the little tenant house and stood, shyly, on their own side of the County Road watching the Braeside folks assembled about the store steps.

Their faces and slippers shone with overmuch polishing; they were like pink and blue petaled blossoms springing from the ditch beside the swale; and their heads were one and all alike, balls of silken, golden floss. One Buckle had a necklace of coral beads about her little throat, and one had a knot of rosy Long-purples tucked under her sweet chin. And they one and all smelled to high heaven of pink geranium soap, Fan having been generous beyond all expectations.

Behind the six small Buckles came Mrs. Buckle with a spotless Skipper swinging from one hand, and a happy Ol' Love from the other. And beside Rosalove walked Piet, proud and handsome in Charles's best blue suit.

"Princesses, huh," scoffed Mr. Hanley turning for a peep across his shoulder while he was struggling with the lock of the store door. "Here we go to all the trouble of traveling to The Center to look at a couple or three of the Dutch kind, when we've got a whole flock of north country beauties right across the road," he added, lifting his voice so that nobody should mistake his opinion. "Good day to you, ma'am, a fair treat for the eyes."

And with that the huddle of Braeside folks around the store steps became distinctly clamorous. They waved, they beckoned, and they cried out, some in trumpet tones and some in thin little piercing shrieks.

"Ahoy, mates!" That was the deep, trumpet call of Captain Todd. Fan and George saluted gravely.

"Delia darling!" Mrs. Mold's gentle voice might be overlooked in the uproar by some, but not by Delia Buckle. She held out both small arms and threw Mrs. Mold a kiss across the County Road.

"Adabracadabra!" Mr. Liggard's greeting was far deeper and much louder than the captain's. It rumbled more. And little Horace danced in the dust, giggling excitedly.

"Piet! Ol' Love! Piet!" Mrs. Moom leaned past Prissy and opened wide the door of her car. "Oh, you all look so sweet, dears. No prettier blossoms ever grew in Braeside."

"Hi, Eddy!" boomed Mr. Hooke.

A good many eyes and ears around the store that day could hardly believe what they were seeing and hearing, remembering what took place there the week before. Particularly when Miss Tissy Binns pushed to the front and waved her parasol to attract attention.

"Eddy! Piet! Eddy!" she shrieked. The same thin, piercing shriek everybody recognized at once but with different, far different words. "Look behind you. That old pest of an Oliver Binns is running all over your trailer and making a perfect nuisance of himself. Chase him off, Eddy. Give him a good clip on the ears. My, how nice you all look. Even Mark." She was not the first one to notice this, but she was the first one to comment on Mark's appearance. "A straw sun hat tied under his chin with pink ribbons." She was only saved from tittering by Mrs. Witchit's warning hand on her elbow. "And a bunch of Long-purples fastened to the brim. My, my, my!"

"Charles," cried Mrs. Witchit. "Won't you come with us in the station wagon? We all want you, dear."

We all want you! Those were the four words that made this day pleasant. Braeside knew the Buckles, and wanted them. "But we couldn't come over there with you yet," Fan piped suddenly. "Not until we've all been invited."

"Fan, lovey."

The Buckles, as one, turned reproving glances on the mite in the pink sunsuit and coral beads. Before a word

could be uttered, however, everybody felt the County
Road shudder and thud under their feet. Heard, too, the
horrible crashing, clatter, and banging beyond the bend
where the white birch trees grew. None of the Braeside
folks questioned the meaning of the thunderous racket
this time. They knew it wasn't an earthquake, or gun fire
at Pine Camp, or blasting across the Border where the new
King's Highway was being laid out. They knew it was
Mr. Watson's tractor.

Mr. Watson was back from Gananoque.

Mr. Watson was home again and he was coming with
Jim and the tractor to pull the Buckles away from Braeside.

"Boy-y-y, if we don't have the worst luck with our Holidays," said Fan, speaking this time for all those Buckles.

The tractor coughed twice and stopped. All the folks
that were gathered around the store steps saw Jim climb
out and begin fussing with the engine. Mr. Watson's car,
however, passed the tractor and moved right along to
Braeside. Mr. Buckle was driving, Mr. Watson sat beside him, and a woman was alone in back. That is, she
was alone in the back of Mr. Watson's car until she
reached the store and then it seemed as if she blew right
through the side door without waiting for it to be opened
and made for Mr. Moom with both arms outstretched.

"Oh, darling. Darlings," she cried. And to say that Mr.
Moom was startled is to put the case mildly. "Thank God,
you are here," she added, spinning Mr. Moom around by

the elbow and shoving him aside as if he had been nothing more important than a paper doll. "My darlings, my darlings. Ol' Love! Piet! Ol' Love, sweet!"

"It's Mom," clamored Rosalove and Piet, pushing Mr. Moom quite out of the way in quite another direction. "Mom found us."

Fan was enraged at such ingratitude. "It was Eddy Buckle that found you," she snapped from her refuge behind Captain Todd's knee. "If it hadn't been for Eddy you might have been a petunia to this very minute."

Nobody listened. Nobody cared about the finder, now. Here they all were, together again, and that was enough. But not for Fan Buckle. "Mr. Watson," she shouted above the turmoil. "Eddy fetched Ol' Love an' Piet right out of a flower show. He got first prize for that old black cat on our trailer, but he didn't get anything for Ol' Love an' Piet. Only he brought 'em home just the same."

"I'm not surprised," said Mr. Watson, who always listened to Fan. He stepped out of his car, sat down on the store steps, and shoved his hat to the back of his head. "Eddy is quite a lad for bringing things home."

"He couldn't find Ol' Love's Aunty Penelope Paxton, though."

"Penelope Paxton," shrilled Mrs. Mold suddenly. Everybody was startled. Mrs. Mold was such a sad, quiet little woman. The Braeside folks didn't know that she could speak above a whisper, hardly. And here she was, crying out like Miss Tissy Binns or Fan Buckle at their best. "Penelope—Penelope Paxton!" she repeated. "Why, I am Penelope Paxton. And you," she threw both arms around the strange woman and drew her close to her face, "you are my own dear little sister Delia who went to live in Dover. To think that I didn't even know you at first."

"We've both changed with the years, Penelope darling."

"Changed?" gasped Fan, stepping out into the County Road the better to see. "You haven't changed any, Mrs. Mold," she said firmly. "You are still Mrs. Mold."

"But once, when I was a little girl, I was Penelope Paxton," Mrs. Mold replied, to the surprise of all. "Delia and I lived with our Grandmother Paxton on the old Cape Vincent Road. Then after Grandmother died we were separated."

"We know all about that," Fan told her smugly. "We got the angels to bring together those who were separated, but they wouldn't have had such a hard time about it if she had put 'Penelope Mold' on Ol' Love's tag. Why didn't she?"

"Mold?" repeated the strange woman, pressing her slender fingertips against her eyes. "Mold? I seemed to forget so many things when the bomb dropped among the roses on Freel's garden clock."

"Mom was shocked," Piet explained gently, reaching for her hand. "She was a long time under care. But she will be quite all right here in Braeside. It's almost like Dover,

Mom. Blue water and wheeling terns, lovely gardens, a yew cock."

"But what I want to know," Mrs. Mold interrupted suddenly, "is why somebody around here didn't tell me that these children were looking for an Aunty Penelope Paxton."

"I wouldn't let 'em," Delia Buckle confessed sadly. "I told the folks that it made you cry so to think about the war and for them to wait until Mr. Watson got back. We knew that Mr. Watson would find Ol' Love's Aunty just as soon as he came."

"An' boy-y-y, if he didn't," said Fan proudly.

Once again there was a thudding underfoot and a clash, clatter, and bang at the bend in the road.

"Jim's started the engine," said Mr. Watson, standing up and waving toward the trailer. "All aboard, everybody who wants to leave the swale for drier parts. Abijah and I discovered a good place for a new home out beyond River-head."

Fan threw herself against Captain Todd's best blue suit and buzzed like a gnat. "No, no, no," she said over and over again. "Tell him no, sir."

"No," replied Captain Todd and, surprisingly enough, Mr. Moom in one and the same firm voice. Nobody had appealed to Mr. Moom, but that seemed to make little difference.

"No," they repeated in chorus. "You won't move that tenant house away from Braeside unless you want to lose every friend you've got this side of The Center, Watson."

Mr. Watson sat down on the store steps again. "Do you mean to tell me, after last week, that you want all these Buckles, the whole alphabet from A to N——"

"Q," Captain Todd corrected him. "We put Q after S-is-Skipper so as to hold the situation well in hand. No more alphabet after S-is-Skipper."

"Of course we want all these Buckles in Braeside," added Mr. Moom. "We've never laughed so much in a hundred years. And Eddy's got a job here, as soon as he gets around to it."

"Gorry, come to think of it, you can't move them away from here, Watson." Captain Todd's voice lifted above the others. "Fan and I did a piece of magic a few days ago. Wished on a lily, that's what we did. You can't go against anything like that, you know."

"Yes, you can, I mean, yes, he can," cried Fan, leaving the shelter of the captain's knee to attach herself to Mr. Watson's pocket. "You can go a little ways against it. Just enough to let us live up there on your hillside. An alphabet should live on a hillside, you know. Up against the pines where we had a Holiday while you were gone. You could build us a long white house up there with a porch in front where we could sit an' look right down into Braeside, an' see whenever Captain Todd takes THE MOLLY out into Lily Bay, an' whenever Mrs. Mold trims her white roses, an' whenever Mr. Liggard puts a new story stick in his garden, an' whenever Mr. Moom clips the cock."

"Gad, what a nosy kid you've got here, Abijah," said Mr. Watson. Fan denied the charge hotly.

"I'm not nosy," she said. "Only Braeside is the nicest place in all the world."

"Since when, pink dot? If I remember correctly it was only last week that you said——"

"Oh-h, last week." Fan flicked the affairs of last week aside with a wave of her hand. "We weren't acquainted around here then," she explained airily. "Mother always tells us that folks are almost sure to like each other if they get to know each other real well, only it's better to go slow an' not force your acquaintance on strangers. An' that's just what we did. Boy-y-y, did we go slow! But after a while we were all invited to come down Braeside. That is, we were all invited except——"

"Fan, sweety."

"Yes'm." Fan choked and hid her face in her mother's skirt. "I wasn't hinting," she muttered proudly, "I was just telling him."

"All right," said Mr. Watson. "Then tell me why I shouldn't pull the little tenant house down Braeside and plant it on my vacant lot on the bank above the dock."

It was Miss Tissy Binns, of all people, who told him. "I'm ashamed of you, Mark Watson, to even think of locating all these Buckles on that spot of ground," she snapped. "That big white house on the hillside is the smartest idea I've heard yet. There would be plenty of room for them up against the pines, and they would still be near us. We need them near us, Mark Watson. Milly Witchit could never manage her oil stove without Charles, and we have just begun to learn how to 'sacker-fize,' and we are all regular customers of Eddy's. I know what. Why not build the house on the hillside for the Buckles, and move this little tenant house down on the vacant lot next to me for Piet's family? It would just about fit them, with a little touching up. Then we would all be together."

"Gad," said Mr. Moom, climbing into the station wagon. "Here's something I want to see through. Take the other cars, any of the rest of you who would rather go to The Center and watch that parade. This one is going to be good enough for me."

The Braeside parade, it seemed, was good enough for everybody. Nobody even turned an eye toward The Center. "After we have led the little tenant house down the street to its new home, let's collect all the food we had prepared for supper tonight," said Mrs. Liggard, "and take it over to the vacant lot and have a real old-fashioned shore dinner on the bank above the river." And that was an idea that struck everyone as the second best one yet.

"I haven't been to a shore dinner in more than ten years," said Mrs. Moom. She wasn't white as the dove on Freel's clock any more. Her cheeks were pink with excitement. "Help me out of this car for a minute, Prissy," she whispered. And then, crossing the County Road while

Jim was busy again with the tractor engine, she laid her hand on Mrs. Buckle's arm and said, "I haven't time to make it a written invitation now, my dear, but will you allow us to welcome you to Braeside and to our friendship as we have welcomed your family? Will you forget last week forever, and will you ride in the station wagon with Mr. Moom and me at the head of the parade? Please say you will."

Mrs. Buckle chuckled, tucked Skipper under her arm, and crossed the County Road.

"Law me, that's the very last invitation we needed," said Fan contentedly. "Where's George?"

George, it seemed, had led the scramble up the orange boxes as soon as Jim was ready to back the tractor into the swale. He was now sitting in the opened doorway of the little kitchen and he was very, very busy. His best coat was gone. So was his white shirt and stiff collar. So was his necktie. And he was now entirely occupied with a tight, polished shoe. Fan needed no explanation.

"Boy-y-y, is that a good idea," she buzzed. "Delia, toss out my old sneaks too, will you? I'm taking off these buckled slippers."

The Braeside parade would never be forgotten. Mr. Moom led it in the station wagon with Mrs. Moom, Mrs. Buckle, and Skipper.

Behind, in the second station wagon, rode the Liggards, the Molds with Mom, and Captain Todd.

They were followed by the car that was driven by Mr. Hooke. Mrs. Hooke, Miss Tissy Binns, and Mrs. Witchit rode with him and were noisily merry every foot of the way.

Next came Mr. Watson, Abijah Buckle, and Mr. Hanley from the store.

And then Jim with the tractor and all the men from the farm.

Behind the tractor was the trailer and the little tenant house and all the Buckles in a golden ring, with Ol' Love as their guest.

Imogene stumbled lazily along behind the trailer.

And behind Imogene went Mark, already bored by his new straw hat and its floppy Long-purple decoration.

Mark was followed, of course, by Nero, with Eddy's golden head and Piet's dark fuzz barely showing above the fat man in the pink nightgown.

And last of all, not too happy about being mixed up in the whole affair but fearing to miss any of it, strolled Oliver Binns still faintly redolent of sardines.

No, this parade would never be forgotten by any of the Braeside folks, at least.

Nor the afternoon that followed.

While they ate they all took a hand in planning the long white house that was to be built against the pines on the lovely hillside. Mr. Watson told Jim and Fred and Chuck to round up a gang of workmen in The Center the very next day and see that the new house blossomed as fast as another daisy in the field of dogbane and purple vetch.

"We've got to hurry," he explained. "The Buckles have got to have a roof over their heads before Eddy begins bringing home any more alphabet. I wouldn't trust that lad, Q or no Q. You're going to hear plenty of banging around here, folks."

"Good," cried Mrs. Witchit. "I can hardly wait." She pressed a second quarter of lemon pie on Mr. Watson and cut into the fresh huckleberry for Charles. "Where are all these good people going to spend the next few nights?"

"The Buckles at the farm," Mr. Watson told her before anybody else could speak. "And Piet's folks with the Molds, I take it."

"Oh, yes." Mrs. Mold left no doubt in anybody's mind about that. "We'll want to plan about the little tenant house."

"After me, my dear lady," Mr. Watson interrupted firmly. "Abijah and I will round up another gang of workmen in Riverhead tomorrow for work on that tenant house. Let's see, the place could do with three bedrooms at least."

"An' doors," Eddy reminded him. "Golly, the things that have poked in an' crawled over me nights."

"An' don't forget a porch in front." Fan put down a wedge of chocolate cake to add her bit. "When Ol' Love's father comes back from Dunkirk he'll want to sit out there with Mom, like Mr. and Mrs. Moom do, an' watch the gulls over Jackstraw Lighthouse."

"We mustn't forget the garden." Miss Tissy turned her back on the river and considered the ground around the little tenant house. "This lot has been neglected long enough. It's the only weedy spot in Braeside."

"It won't be much longer," chuckled Mr. Hooke. "That's something we can get at tomorrow morning. I'll spade a good wide border over there, about in line with that patch of daisies."

"And I'll lay out a nice little herb garden in one end of it," said Miss Tissy happily. "Lavender, rosemary, sage, thyme, and the savories. I've got plenty of roots to spare."

"And I've got a splendid bittersweet vine for the corner of the porch," Mrs. Witchit pointed out the corner she meant, "if there was only somebody to do the digging. Bittersweet roots pretty deep, but it would be lovely against those silvery gray shingles."

"What's the matter with my good right arm, Milly?" asked Captain Todd, as pleasantly as though his little girl hadn't married Mrs. Witchit's boy and gone away to live in Detroit. "I was aiming to fork up a little vegetable garden for Mom out in back there, but that can come later. Just toss a call across the hedge when you want the vine moved."

Mrs. Mold patted her sister's hand lovingly. "Do you remember those little white roses you used to grow?" she whispered. "We'll scatter them all over the place."

"And I," said Mr. Liggard with a knowing wink at little Horace, "not to be outdone in this garden business, shall shake my magic handkerchief over the whole plot and you may expect to find silver bells, cockle shells, and pretty maids wherever you look."

Horace put down his cherry tart and moved closer to his own personal magician, adoring him with wide blue eyes.

Nobody paid any attention to the time. Braeside was having too much fun at its first picnic in years and years and years. They might have remained there on the bank above the river all night, nibbling at this and that, chatting about the past and future, growing friendlier and friendlier, if it had not been for Mrs. Moom. When she hopped to her feet, brushing the crumbs out of her lap, everybody stood up with her.

"Look," she said, pointing toward Lily Bay. "I always come outside at this time in the afternoon and stand where I can watch the sun plop down among the lilies out there, like a great red balloon. See, it has just touched the water now. And all the gentle ripples are turning rosy. And the sky above is flaming red as the sun ball drops down, down, down into the Bay. In a minute the red will fade to a pale lavender, and then there will be long, trailing wisps of delicate green scudding along the sky. And when the last rim of the sun has disappeared——"

"It will be the end of one of the happiest days we have ever known in Braeside, my dear," said Mr. Moom. "And we'll all go home to get ready for another one. I don't mind telling you, boys and girls, that the Cliffton Bank and all my committees are going to get along without me tomorrow. I've got more important work to attend to right here at home. Ol' Love and I are going to clip the hedge around this lot, and we'll have a yew peacock beside the gate, by golly, or my name's not Moom."

Fan Buckle slept in a real bed that night for the first time since leaving the dear old farm that the army took for an airfield. It was a little white bed with a pink silk puff thrown across the foot and on any other evening Fan, buzzing with excitement over it, would have had the whole alphabet in for a look. Tonight, however, there was a little matter of business between herself, God, and the good angels that needed her full attention. She knelt at the foot of the little white bed and pressed her cheek against the pink silk puff as she prayed.

"Dear God, angels, an' everybody up in heaven," she whispered, "You'll all have to help now, 'cause there are two houses to be built in a hurry. One is on a hillside an' that's for us, an' one is down in Braeside on the vacant lot an' that's for Ol' Love. An' why You've got to hurry is that Ol' Love is going to miss me like everything, an' Piet an' Eddy have just got around to earning puh-len-ty of money for the poor people over where the war is now that Mark has got his strength back an' everybody's a regular customer. We thought Mr. Watson could get us a place to live in a day, but it's been a week now, so You've got to help him. Thank You for helping Eddy bring together those who were separated. And thank You for the Holiday we had today. That was the very best Holiday we ever had anywhere. Pies an' choc'late cakes an' roz'b'ry sandwiches till you couldn't see, an' no tight shoes, or neckties, or Aunty Belles to it either. Only help Mr. Watson along with those two houses. An', oh yes, thank You for making the Braeside folks say 'God bless all those Buckles!' Yes, they did. That's just exactly what they said an' was *I* surprised, too! Amen."